IARRAI

Also by Philip Dickens

FROM THE HILL OF MEGIDDO

Armageddon's Offspring Series
ORPHANS OF THE DEAD
SINS OF THE ANGELS

IARRAINDORN

PHILIP DICKENS

Friendly Badger Publishing
Pontypridd, Wales

www.friendly-badger.com

This paperback edition 2021
1

First published globally by
Friendly Badger Publishing 2021

ISBN: 9798712785100

Cover Art © 2021 Keira James
www.keirajamesart.com

For Dee. I could ask for no better cheerleader and enabler.
I love you to the moon and back. x

ABOUT THE AUTHOR

Philip Dickens lives in Pontypridd with his wife Dee, daughter-person Noah, and their two shy and loving but utterly demented cats.

As well as writing supernatural horror fantasy stories, he makes videos on YouTube and livestreams on Twitch. You can find him on both platforms, and other social media, under the handle AKblackandred.

In his spare moments, he has a full-time job where he is a trade union representative for the PCS Union and enjoys helping his fellow workers take on the bosses. (Unfortunately, instead he spends most of his time in meetings.)

Outside of writing, content creation and trade unionism, he enjoys reading stories set in other worlds, watching movies about superheroes and playing computer games involving the indiscriminate slaughter of the undead.

Dee, Noah and their two cats are his whole world.

You can find him online at philipdickens.com

PROLOGUE

The full moon called a hail of stars down from the sky on the night the devil came.

The wind blew with a force that made walking against it not unlike trying to push a boulder uphill. It sent the rain, sharp and cold, straight at you so that it stung where it hit bare flesh, almost as hard as if it were hail. This would have made it hard to see anything, even had the moon not already been buried by the thick, dark clouds. There was no clear divide between the sky and the land, the whole of it being draped in a shroud of black without end.

Two druids stood watch. The thick fur lining their robes were soaked through and clinging to their bodies, any warmth it may have provided substituted for weight which pulled their shoulders down and pushed their boots into the mud. Their thick beards were a mass of knots and tangles, while their long hair clung to their cheeks and foreheads, under cowls which may as well have not been there for all the protection they offered from the elements.

Each wore a knot of holly around the wrist of their right hand, and held a long staff topped by oil-soaked rags. The flames there fought bravely, constantly threatening to gutter out but still offering one tiny refuge of light and warmth against the fury of the elements. For all the good that it did.

Ahead of them, unseen in the unending veil of darkness, the river had broken its banks. The water crashed and swelled, foaming over the land, churning grass into mud and reaching out to drag the unwary away in the tide.

From behind them, a third robed druid passed through the line of four very old birch trees laden with mistletoe that marked the start of the village. He too carried a staff with a struggling flame at its head, but he was also leading a ram which struggled against its leash in protest at being dragged from the dry warmth of the barn.

"Will one be enough?" One of the two druids already standing watch said as the third came close enough for the weak flames to illuminate him.

"One is always enough." The third snapped. "Judoc may be fond of needless extravagance, but the gods ask for a gift, not for the depletion of our livestock."

Lightning flashed in the sky, making the rain appear to shine. Two seconds later, thunder rolled across the sky, a drawn-out rumble ending in an almighty crash. The ram bleated in panic and the three druids shared a dark look.

"With this weather, how are we to know when the signs present themselves?"

"We will know. Signs are meant to be seen. The gods would not hide them away."

"Let's get on with it then."

The first two druids lifted their staffs up, with some effort since their limbs were cold and stiff. They chanted in unison, a prayer to the goddess of the flooded pool for her protection, though even at this close range all that the third druid could hear was a low muttering from which individual words were hard to distinguish. He watched, waiting for them to finish and lower their arms.

When they did, he raised his own staff and said his own prayer. This one was addressed to the god of the forest, and again to his two companions his words sounded like nothing more than a low mutter.

Their prayers were straightforward enough. For strength from the river, for protection from the forest, and for wisdom from both. Nothing too extravagant or out of the ordinary, but of course the gods' price could not be paid in gold or favours. Blood was needed.

The ram kicked and cried out as the bronze blade was drawn across its throat. But the struggle didn't last long. The blood poured out black onto the already sodden ground, but enough of it fell into cupped hands for the purposes of offering. A bloody handprint on the trunk of each birch in turn, and then two blood stained hands pressed into the mud to be washed clean by the river, and it was done. The gods had their blood, and a family would have a meal to celebrate the arrival of their newest member.

"We've done what we can."

"Let's hope it's enough."

Lightning split the sky once more. This time the thunderclap was almost immediate. The wind still threw it straight into their faces, but now the rain began to lessen, if only slightly. Looking up, the three men could see starlight breaking through gaps in the cloud cover. It was the closest they would come to a calm in the storm, but it was enough to see the sign that they had been waiting for.

A line of stars streaked across the sky, trailing fire in their wake. They made no sound, or at least none that reached human ears, rushing silently across the black and cutting the darkness to shreds. In the flashes of lightning, they had been able to make out the shape of the horizon and distinguish where the water ended and the land began, but everything had still been grey and shadow. Now, it was as though the sun was still only three quarters down and they could see their surroundings clearly. That was how they saw the newcomers.

There were ten of them, just as sodden with rain as the

druids, their tunics and trousers clinging heavy to them and the short spikes of their hair flattened under the weight of water. But if they felt the chill of the cold, they did not show it. Indeed, it wouldn't be clear how they could when their faces weren't human.

Their eyes glowed red and their skin was drawn and grey. Their lips peeled back from their gums, revealing teeth that were pointed like arrowheads. The skin around their nails had receded where the nails had grown into sharp claws. Yet for their monstrous appearance, they stood like men. They wore swords on their hips and most had one clawed hand at their side, ready to draw their weapon.

The druids drew closer together, but if they were afraid, they did not show it. Instead, they reached out with the arms bearing the knot of holly and spoke in unison.

"You are not welcome here, dark creatures. Be gone from this place. In the name of Brigantia, in the name of the goddess of the flooded pool and the god of the forest, we implore you. Be gone from this place. For the high ones and the old ones, we expel you. Be gone!"

The creatures looked at one another and then back at the druids. After a moment's pause, they burst out laughing. The sound wouldn't have been out of place in a long hall, where somebody had told a bawdy joke and all the listeners had drunk too many horns of ale, except for the added measure of threat behind the creatures' mirth.

The show in the skies ended, and with the disappearance of the falling stars the entire landscape was plunged into darkness. Within moments, screams rose in the night air.

The village wasn't particularly big. There were twenty houses, round walls topped by conical thatched roofs, the smallest walled with wooden poles and the largest with stone. Fires burned inside them all, where people huddled in furs against the biting cold outside. But the lights in the sky had brought people to their doors to gawk at the strange signs.

"Caiside!" A voice called from inside one of the houses, the voice sharp, both angry and pained.

Caiside turned from the doorway, shamefaced, to look at his wife. Genovefa sat on a pile of furs close to the fire, sweating, red faced and clutching at her massively swollen belly. Two of the elder women gathered around her supported her back while a third was in front of her with water and blankets. All of them had the same look of disdain on their faces. With one last look at the sky, he made his way back over to the fire.

The labour had so far been a slow and painful one, and the baby hadn't yet even begun to crown. It had been light when Genovefa had first doubled over in pain, and Caiside had sought out the elders to tend to her. He had been beset by panic then, not really knowing what to do, and though that had subsided it had only left him feeling useless; unable to do anything to help, unable to even try without getting a stern telling off from whichever woman he had gotten in the way of, but unable to leave because his wife wanted him by her side. He hadn't the slightest idea why, since he had no role whatsoever, but she was a ferocious woman at the best of times and the pregnancy had hardly tempered that. Especially as it wore on.

For her part, her husband's feelings of uselessness were the least of Genovefa's worries. She was panting heavily, building herself up to the next push and the agony that would come with it. She had felt nothing like it before. Her friends who had given birth had said that the only comparable combination of exertion and pain would be on a battlefield, and now she knew exactly what they meant. She pushed, and with the pushing gave an almighty cry.

She heard the screams just as her own cries died down. They were faint and distant, but it was clear enough what they were. She shared a look with Caiside, and it was clear that he had heard them as well.

"Well?" She snapped. "See what it is!"

With that, he hurried back to the doorway and looked out once more. There wasn't much to see now, since the lights in the sky had gone and left only darkness in their wake. But the people who had been looking up from the doorways had now stepped out into the open air. Several of the warriors had gathered outside the long hall, with swords drawn, while the farmers and fishermen wielded their sickles and harpoons.

Following the screams, though, silence fell. A minute or so passed in darkness as everybody waited, tense. Then lightning struck over the river and the deep boom of the thunder made everybody jump, provoking some nervous laughter.

Something flew through the air and landed with a soft splat in the mud in the middle of the village. Caiside couldn't see what it was, just a small round shape in the near distance, but when two more shapes landed with their own splat sounds, his imagination filled in the gaps in his knowledge.

"Who goes there?" Elisedd, the town chief, called. "Show yourself!" He thrust his sword at the empty air as though to underline his command.

Flames erupted on the four trees at the entrance to the village, in moments turning the ancient birch into great torches that threw the darkness back. The rain had reduced to almost nothing now, so that the fire held its ground easily. But no sooner had everybody turned to look at the burning trees than their eyes were drawn back to the three objects that had landed in the mud.

As Caiside had feared, they were heads. The last expressions marked on the druids' faces were of fear, which was now mirrored on the faces of all the other villagers, including the warriors.

Elisedd was the first to school his expression and stepped forward boldly. "You mean to scare us with your gesture?" He roared. "It is clearly you who are scared, hiding in the shadows and confronting us with tricks rather than with iron! Show yourselves!"

Whatever came at Elisedd moved too fast to see clearly. Caiside heard a growl, a sound he would attribute to a wolf or a wild dog, full of hunger and menace. But the shape that came into the open was too big to be either. He could have sworn that it was a man, not only from its size and stride but because even as a blur it looked as though it was clothed. But it moved far too fast, charging straight at Elisedd and goring him so that both he and his attacker landed several feet back from the long hall.

That first attacker wasn't alone, and his companions gave the village no time to take in what they had seen. Elisedd's landing was immediately followed by cries and screams as more attackers came. Caiside couldn't see from where. They seemed able to take impossible leaps as well as charge as fast as wild animals, and shortly the middle of the village was overtaken by a pitched battle. Men ran this way and that, wrestled on the ground, or swung their swords. The enemy seemed to be everywhere, and they had swords of their own. Cries of anger and fear and pain sang out over the crash of iron against iron, and Caiside knew that he was far out of his depth.

He stumbled back inside his house, where Genovefa was pushing again and along with the women attending her seemed oblivious to the carnage outside. The baby's head was visible now, he saw, pink and covered in blood. He should have been proud, becoming a father, but this only made the situation even more impossible.

"The village is under attack!" He cried, as if it made any difference when they were in no position to move.

"The Cornovii?" One of the attending women asked.

He shook his head. "I don't know who they are. They're not... they're..." He shook his head again.

Between pushes, panting heavily, Genovefa said, "Arm yourself. Watch the door."

He nodded, not knowing what else to do. Part of him

suspected that right now his wife presented a more fearsome threat to any potential invader than he did. Still, he grabbed a scythe and made for the door.

As he looked outside, he saw Elisedd swing his sword and take the head of one of the attackers. He caught the chief's eye as the severed head fell to the ground, and in that instant felt more confident about the situation. That confidence evaporated in an instant when another attacker landed on the chief's back, his weight driving Elisedd down to his knees, and sunk sharp teeth into his neck.

Seeing blood, bright and visceral under the orange glow of the flames, Caiside felt bile rise in his throat. He swallowed it down when he saw the creature's face, that of a corpse and a monster all at once. His heart stopped and his legs felt weak under him. Every instinct was crying out at him to flee for his life, but he swallowed them down and raised the scythe, ready to strike if the thing came at him.

This turned out to be unnecessary, as Elisedd head butted the creature, which tore a chunk from his neck as it fell backwards. The chief turned his cry of pain into a battle cry as he forced himself up and stabbed it in the heart.

This didn't stop the creature growling and squirming, so Elisedd drew his sword out of the thing's chest and brought it down sharply on its neck.

"Take their heads!" He cried to the other warriors. "That's the only way to kill them! Take their heads!"

Looking around, Caiside could see that the monsters were on the back foot now. Despite their fearsome appearance, and whatever abilities they possessed, the warriors were routing them and only six of them still stood – they were outnumbered and would soon enough be finished.

Or so he thought, until he saw their leader.

It emerged from the shadows, and it was unclear how long it had been there as he was sure that he would have noticed it before now. It stood well over eight-foot-tall, with eyes that glowed red and long, curved horns protruding from the sides of its head. A pair of leathery wings protruded from its back, as broad as the creature was tall. It carried no weapons, and even as it stepped out into the light cast by the fire on the trees shadow wreathed its form so that Caiside could make out no features on its face or body.

A warrior, fresh from decapitating one of the lesser monsters, turned and swung his sword at the beast. It caught the blade easily with one hand and then, with a flick of its wrist, snapped it in half as if it were made of wood. With another flick of its wrist, it sent the warrior flying and carried on walking as though the interruption had never occurred.

It was heading straight towards Caiside.

Elisedd put himself between Caiside and the beast, sword at the ready, but this was scant comfort given what it had just done. As it stepped closer, with no urgency whatsoever as though it were simply out on a mid-afternoon stroll, Caiside's heartbeat grew faster and thundered through his ears.

"Adversary! Halt!"

The shout came from over by the burning trees. When Caiside turned, he was sure that he was seeing things, even with the enormous monster approaching his house. For he was looking at a woman with two enormous, feathery white wings on her back. She had golden brown hair that hung to her shoulders and brown skin that glowed slightly, unnaturally, in the darkness. She wore light plate armour over tunic and trousers and was wielding a longsword.

"Anael." The creature said, simply, as it turned to face her. "How nice of you to join us."

"You won't have him." Anael said, advancing upon the creature. "Leave this place."

The beast's laughter was a deep and terrible sound, like thunder. "And you will stop me, archangel? Please do try."

"Did you think I wouldn't have prepared for your

arrival?"

She pressed the blade of her sword against her opposite palm and drew blood. In one quick motion she pulled her cut hand away and thrust it in the air towards the monster. Her blood flew from her wrist and hit the ground, whereupon the churned-up mud bubbled and smoked, before erupting in green flames. The unnatural fire rushed in a straight line towards the enormous winged monster, whereupon it encircled him, trapping him where he stood.

This drew a snarl from the monster.

Anael responded with a smirk. "You are not welcome here, father of evil. You are unwanted. I cast you out and I ward this place against you so that you may never set foot here again. On behalf of the entire host and in the name of Our Father, I cast you out. Ahriman, you are expelled. Be gone!"

She raised and clenched her fist, and the circle of green flame drew tighter around the beast, like a noose. Before it could engulf the creature, however, it vanished as though it had never stood there. But as it vanished its voice echoed all around.

"You cannot stop me. Eventually, the Champion's life will be mine and the seals will be broken."

For several moments, Caiside forgot to breathe. He wasn't the only one. All around, villagers stared with mouths open and eyes wide, and no idea how to comprehend what they had just seen. Even the remaining other monsters had been forgotten, except by the warriors who had been fighting them, and in the stunned silence following the defeat of their master the four surviving creatures fled the village.

Then cheers erupted, and Caiside found himself waving his scythe in the air and bellowing in relief and joy.

As Anael made her way through the raucous villagers to Caiside's house, Caiside showered her with thanks. "You have saved our village! My life – those men, that creature, such darkness! I don't know how to thank you…"

As he babbled at her, she made her way into his house, where she found Genovefa sitting holding his new-born son, while the attending women looked on. The baby was wrapped in furs and gurgling as she rocked him gently in her arms and sang at him. Genovefa looked up and met Caiside's eyes with a tired smile, before looking at the winged woman.

"You'll have to forgive my husband." She said. "He is overcome with excitement. From what I heard, you saved the village, and so our son. You have our thanks."

Anael smiled and knelt at the side of the new mother and child. She wiggled her fingers in the baby's face and he giggled.

"Your son is very important." Anael said to Genovefa. "Your village was attacked because The Great Adversary wants him dead, to stop him from fulfilling his destiny. I am here to protect him and train him, so that he will fulfil it. My name is Anael."

Genovefa looked at Caiside, who was as bewildered by what had happened as anybody and could only shrug. Then she looked back at Anael. "My father used to say that destiny was just a word some men used to justify their domination and murder of other men."

"Your father was a wise man." Anael lifted the baby's hand and turned it so they could all see the red mark on his thumb in the shape of a dagger. "But your son will be a Champion of Man."

Genovefa didn't look convinced, but she nodded. "If you being here means that my son will be safe from whatever attacked our village, then I can worry about destinies at some later date. But – if you are to live here in our village as one of us," she gestured at Anael's wings, "you will have to look less…conspicuous."

"I think I can manage that." Anael said, laughing.

"Then you should meet your Champion." Genovefa lifted the baby up and presented him to Anael. "His name will be Nuadhu."

ACT ONE:
EARNING A NAME

CHAPTER ONE

The only sounds to be heard in the early morning as the sun rose over Liuerpwl were the light rustling of the trees in the breeze, a few birds singing and occasionally a dog barking in excitement as its master rose. As the villagers finished breaking their fasts and prepared to start the day's work, soon the quiet would be overtaken, but for now Anael took the opportunity to enjoy it.

"CHAAAAAAAAAAAAARRRRGGGGGEEEEEEE!"

The war cry was followed by cheers and giggles as Nuadhu led a small horde of children stamping through the village. Several loose chickens scattered in their wake, clucking in alarm. The children all carried branches or sticks, which they waved about ahead of them as they ran, and several of the very youngest kept stumbling in the charge.

Once they reached the open grassland just past the blackened husks of the four birches that had marked the start of the village, they turned and started to fight among themselves. Nearly all of them swung at their opponents' sticks rather than at their opponents themselves, shouting and laughing as their weapons clashed. The older ones had the sense not to fight with the younger ones, and a couple of boys no older than four moved around and swung their small sticks at the backs of the older children.

One of these younger boys was Nuadhu's brother Pwyll. The two of them looked alike, with matching green eyes and wild shocks of red hair on their heads, Nuadhu's hanging to his shoulders and Pwyll's sticking out in all directions as though he had been struck by lightning. But where Pwyll was still small, with a round face and soft belly, already at ten Nuadhu was tall for his age. He had a strong jaw and broad shoulders.

Anael had been patrolling the perimeter of the village. From a short distance away, she watched the children fighting for several moments before heading towards the long hall. Sheathing her sword at her side, she hefted the large sack at her side so that it sat over her shoulder. It was particularly heavy today, the weight pulling backwards and towards the ground as she moved. Still, having had long practice, it gave her no trouble.

Wearing a locally-made chest plate over a simple tunic and trousers, with her hair tied back in a tight braid and no suggestion of wings on her back, only the fact that her skin was darker suggested that Anael might not belong in the village. But everybody there knew her, and she knew all of their names. Several of them waved in greeting as they passed her to go about their day's work. There were others though, mostly older members of the village, who avoided her gaze.

"Anael!" Elisedd called as he stepped out of the long hall. "A good night's work?"

She dropped the sack on the ground and gestured to it. "See for yourself!"

He knelt and opened it to peer inside, grimacing as he did so. There were six severed heads in the sack, all of them with red eyes, grey skin and lips peeled back from pointed teeth. Anael had left the bodies where they had fallen, feed for the crows. Elisedd closed the sack again and stepped back from it.

There were more lines on his face now than when she had first met him, and his short, thick hair might have been showing the first signs of going grey were it not already stripped of colour by the frequent use of lime to bleach it. But he was as stout and strong as ever, a silver torc around his neck the only indicator of his rank.

"Is there no end to these creatures?" He asked.

"As long as there are men, the Sons of Cain can always make more of themselves." Anael said.

"Then we are lucky to have you with us. Come."

He led her into the long hall, now empty. She followed him past the long table and the benches which ran along either side of it, where several serving girls removed empty plates and wiped away spilled food, and up to a second, much smaller table in front of his high seat. He sat and gestured to a stool at his side.

"You must be hungry after a hard night's work."

As she sat down, Anael conceded that she was. So Elisedd had a joint of meat, a bowl of stew and a horn of beer brought out for her. As she ate and drank, Elisedd stared off into the distance, thinking. Clearly something weighed on his mind, but she didn't stop to think about it as she filled herself up. The chief was uncomplicated, and would no doubt divulge what was on his mind soon enough.

"You're set to begin training the boy." He said once she had finished eating. "Have you broached the subject of his destiny yet?"

She shook her head. "He knows that he is being trained to be a Champion of Man. But what that means, and the future it gives him – no, I haven't talked to him about that yet. It's a lot to place on anybody, let alone a child."

"Yes, of course. But he won't be a child for too much longer, and as a man he needs to be prepared for what he will face."

"He will be."

"Good. I'll be frank, Anael. I'm glad to have you here,

not only for the protection you have given us from these Sons of Cain, but for the training that you have given our warriors. We are all the richer for it. But there are others who don't think as I do. They view you and the boy as the reason that we were attacked, and that these creatures continue to threaten us."

Anael thought back to those who avoided her gaze and her company. Overwhelmingly they were older; old enough to remember the night that the Adversary invaded and to have lost people then. Not all of them, by any stretch, but enough.

"The boy did nothing wrong except to be born." Elisedd said, reading the look on her face. "I will not tolerate any harm coming to him, just as I wouldn't to any other of my people. But it doesn't help that he is always the ringleader when there is nuisance and mischief."

"Children always create nuisance and mischief." Anael said. "But my training will teach him the need for discipline as well as strength."

"I hope so, Anael. I want to be able to show that he offers more protection for our village, rather than putting it in greater harm. I expect that you will be able to help me with this."

She nodded. "Of course. But first, I'll need to dispose of last night's spoils."

When he agreed and dismissed her, she stood up and walked out of the long hall the way she had come. Only once she was outside, in the air, did her calm façade fail her. Her arms and legs were trembling, and she had to resist the urge to yell obscenities into the air.

The very idea that Nuadhu could be blamed for the circumstances of his birth appalled her. He was a child, and even if he were more of a handful than many others, she simply couldn't comprehend how anybody could contemplate getting rid of him simply to ease their own unspoken fears. At least it appeared to only be a minority, as far as she could tell.

A dog, little more than a pup, was sniffing at the sack of heads and whining as she came out. It looked up when she stepped close and, appearing to sense her mood, slunk away.

To begin his training, Anael had asked Nuadhu to meet her outside of the village at dawn the next day, on the far side from the river. He arrived on time, which was a promising start, but when he did his younger brother was trailing in his wake.

"Pwyll," she said as gently as she could, "what are you doing here?"

The boy puffed out his chest and said, "I'm here to become a Champion with my brother."

Anael had to suppress a smile. "But there's only one Champion, and that's Nuadhu."

"Well," Pwyll paused for only a heartbeat, "then I'll still be a warrior and fight at his side!"

"Your father wants you to become a farmer, to take after him."

"What did your father want you to be?" Pwyll asked.

The question took Anael completely off guard. "What?"

"Your father – what was his plan for you?"

"I – he – he was very proud of me when I became a warrior."

"But that wasn't what he wanted you to be, at first, was it?" Nuadhu said, with a smile on his face as though he had stumbled upon some great secret.

She willed away the heat in her cheeks and smiled back at him. "What makes you so sure?"

"It's just a guess." He shrugged. "Am I right?"

"You're close." She admitted. "Come on."

They set off into the forest, wading through dense undergrowth, until they came to a small clearing. There wasn't much to it, grass growing around the twisted remains of some long dead tree, but she had discovered it

19

while exploring some years back and made a note then that it might be good as a place to take the Champion away from distractions while training. It seemed a good place to start Nuadhu off.

"Are you going to tell me, then?" He asked as he entered the clearing.

"Tell you what?"

"About your father and what he wanted you to be."

"No. We're here to train you."

This didn't put him off. "I've heard people say that you have wings."

She looked over her shoulders. "Really? Where?"

"They say that you hide them, and this isn't your true form."

"Do they?"

"Is it true?"

"I'll tell you what." She had an extra sword on her belt, which she now drew and presented the hilt of to Nuadhu. "If you can land a single blow, then I will answer one question. Just one, mind, so it'll have to be a good one."

Nuadhu looked at the sword doubtfully. At his side, Pwyll nudged him forward, clearly excited to see a sword fight.

"Won't a sword stroke hurt you?" Nuadhu asked.

Anael drew her own sword. "Don't get ahead of yourself, child, you haven't even swung it yet."

"I'm not a child. I'm a warrior."

"Prove it."

He tested the weight of the sword, unsure of the balance as he lifted it up. It was heavy, and he had never handled a real weapon before, so his grip was shaky. But Nuadhu adjusted to the weight quickly, his still scrawny child's body belying the innate physical strength he held as a Champion of Man.

Once he had a steady grip on the sword, he looked at Anael with a wide grin on his face, pleased with himself. She stepped forward and swung her own blade to strike the tip of his. It tipped rapidly towards the ground, almost taking him with it. Pwyll laughed, until the sound earned a scowl from his elder brother.

"Your first lesson is balance." Anael said. "Even if all you ever use a sword for is to crudely slash at your enemies, you need to be aware of its movements. It is a weight apart from your own body, and if you don't adjust your stance to compensate for your swings, then it will topple you."

He had steadied the sword again. She swung at it once more, this time from the opposite side, and then when he lurched with the sword, she stepped around him and kicked him in the backside, sending him face first to the ground.

"Like so."

More laughter from Pwyll. Nuadhu looked up, snarling and red faced.

"Are you going to try and strike me, then, or just lay there all day?"

Nuadhu pushed himself up off the ground, grabbed the sword and ran at her. She sidestepped him and moved behind him. He let out a war cry in the same manner as when playing with the other children the day before and swung the blade in a wide circle. Anael jumped back from it. She waited for Nuadhu to turn before circling around him.

He swung again. A downward slice, an upward slice, several roughly horizontal arcs, and a few rough thrusts. She dodged them all, not raising her sword at all but moving quickly and easily out of the path of his attacks. This went on for several minutes before finally Nuadhu stopped, panting for breath.

"Your second lesson is calm. Anger slows you down and makes you predictable. You told me of every attack you were going to make whole seconds before it came. It's easy to read the body language of an angry man if you know what you're looking for."

"War isn't calm," Nuadhu said.

"No. But by the time you get to war, most of this should be instinct. Before then, you need to learn to school your emotions and draw your strength from something other than rage."

Nuadhu stared at her, more fatigue than understanding in his face.

By way of a demonstration, she raised her sword and swung. She kept her distance from the two boys, but what they saw had the desired effect. The sword moved in loops, slashes and arcs, singing as it cut through the air. Her body moved with the weapon, each step deliberate, and graceful, a dance. She finished by running up the side of a tree into a back flip, then driving her blade into the ground as she landed. An unnecessary flourish, but one that left the brothers suitably impressed.

"Do you want to be able to do that?"

Both nodded vigorously.

"Then make sure you follow what I say and do what I tell you to."

As they walked back through the forest later in the day, Nuadhu lagged a little behind and snapped a branch off a tree. Then he ran forward and whacked Anael on the arm with it before she had time to react.

"What was that?" She demanded.

"A single blow." He said.

She rolled her eyes. "Very funny. Go on then, what's your question?"

"What are you, if you have wings and can hide them?"

"Ah, clever. If you'd have just asked 'have you got wings' I could have said 'yes' and that's all you'd have known. This way you get a better answer."

"I'm not stupid."

"I should hope not, if you're going to be the Champion of Man."

"You still haven't answered the question."

She smiled. Today was the first time that she had had

any prolonged interaction with Nuadhu, and she was already growing fond of him. "Okay, well I do have wings and I can hide them to look like this because I'm an archangel."

"I don't know what that is."

"Well, that's a different question, isn't it?"

He hit her arm with the stick again. "What's an archangel?"

She laughed. "Okay, from now on only striking a clean blow with a sword during training will get you an answer to a question."

"Fine. But tell me what an archangel is first."

"Very well," she said with a smirk on her face. "We're not from your world and –"

Pwyll cut her off. "You're from the Otherworld? Are you a spirit?"

"Don't be stupid. Spirits can't touch things. She must be a sídhe, because she's beautiful and strong and graceful," Nuadhu said, and Anael found herself blushing. "Can you do magic? How old are you?"

"I'm not a sídhe." She said. "Things aren't quite the way your legends tell them. My home is called Elysium, and we're at war with Pandemonium, which is where demons come from. As Champion of Man you'll play an important role in that war here in your world."

"Oh."

Nuadhu looked thoughtful, trying to absorb this new information. Pwyll looked disappointed, and Anael remembered that his mother's stories about the Otherworld and the sídhe had always captivated him. That he and Nuadhu had both been named for heroes of myth probably helped the fascination.

She put a hand on the younger brother's shoulder. "Just because I'm not a sídhe doesn't mean that they're not out there. There are many mysteries to your world that I don't know, and creatures here that you'll never see in Elysium or Pandemonium."

That seemed enough to put Pwyll at ease, and he grinned. "Can we see your wings then?"

"You've had far more answers already than you should have gotten."

"Come on," Nuadhu intoned in support of his brother. "What do you look like, really? Let us see! Let us see!"

She stopped and looked around. They were still in the forest and away from other eyes, so she leaned down towards them and whispered, "Can you keep a secret?"

Both boys nodded.

"You won't tell anybody?"

They shook their heads.

"Alright then."

She closed her eyes and stretched out her hands. Mentally, she reached deep within herself and drew upon the great reserve of power and energy there. She didn't pull it all up, only a fraction – the psychic equivalent of drawing back a veil to allow a peek at what lay beyond.

To Nuadhu and Pwyll she would appear much the same, except that the brown shade of her skin was now overlaid with a golden glow, which also encompassed the two enormous wings on her back. Anael opened her eyes and smiled at the sight of them both staring at her in awe. Then she clapped her hands together and at once she looked human again.

After continuing to stare at her for several seconds more, they continued out of the forest and back to the village. As they came out of the trees, she heard Pwyll whisper, "I told you she was a spirit."

Nuadhu could see the vein in his father's temple throbbing. Caiside was doing his best to look calm, but he could never hide it from his sons when he was annoyed. Perhaps because he was usually annoyed because of something they had done.

"Pwyll," he said. "I know why being a warrior appeals to you. But life isn't always the way that you want it to be."

"Why not?" Pwyll demanded, sullen.

They were in their house, the fire enveloping them in a drowsy warmth as the night got ever darker outside. Genovefa had hold of Caiside's hand, sitting next to him but saying nothing as he tried to set his youngest son straight.

"Things work a certain way. You can't just 'be' a warrior." He said. "The village needs people to be warriors, but it also needs people to farm the land, to hunt and to fish. It needs us more because we're the ones who keep everyone fed."

"So why do I have to be one of the people who farms instead of one of those who fights? Why can't we choose?"

"Do you think that would work? Every boy wants to be a warrior, not a farmer. If you could choose, then we'd have lots of fights and no food. Do you really think we'd be better off if that were the case?"

"No…" Pwyll said. "So why does Nuadhu get to be a warrior?"

Caiside threw up his hands in exasperation and looked to his wife for support.

"Nuadhu isn't training to be a warrior." Genovefa said. "He's a Champion of Man. It's not the same."

"Why not?"

"Well – warriors fight for the village, and for Brigantia if Judoc calls on them to. They fight other warriors from other tribes who want what we have or have what we want. Nuadhu is going to fight for everyone, against an enemy much greater than other people."

"But. But that sounds dangerous. He's my brother and I need to help him to make sure he wins."

Caiside and Genovefa shared a look of affection. She shifted position so that she could embrace her younger son and comfort him. "That's sweet, my love." She said. "But we need you to help us here. Nuadhu will always be okay."

"Will he, though?"

Pwyll's eyes met Nuadhu's then, and the worry in them made Nuadhu tense up. His back went cold and then a shiver traced up his spine. Would he be okay?

That night, despite being wrapped in furs and full from the evening's meal, Nuadhu was still wide awake when the rest of his family drifted off to sleep. He lay staring up at the ceiling, where the fire cast strange shadows on the thatch. As his eyes grew heavier, they saw the shape of the flames, of birds moving through the sky, and of men marching and waving weapons.

One of these shapes grew larger than the rest, until it was the only shadow on the ceiling. All he could see was the head of a man, but it was no ordinary man. The head was broad and sharp, with the chin jutting out at an angle. It had a horn on either side of the face, curved like the horns of a ram. It had red eyes, lips drawn back from teeth that pointed like daggers and dark red skin the texture of leather.

Nuadhu wasn't sure when what he was seeing had stopped being a shadow and become a clear image, but now the thing had a body as well. Arms ripped with muscle that ended in long claws, thick legs with knees bent backwards, and a body covered in moulded black armour. As it loomed over him it spread the two wings on its back out so that it blotted out the light from the fire.

He looked around him, desperately, but neither Pwyll nor his parents stirred. It was just him, with the beast leering hungrily at him. He tried to cry out, but his throat was hoarse, and no sounds came out. The beast chuckled, a deep rumble, and Nuadhu shrank into his bed.

"Champion." The best said. "A pleasure to meet you at last."

"Who are you?" He managed to croak out.

"Why, I am your Great Adversary! Didn't our dear Anael tell you about me? I am disappointed. Still, I suppose you are young and under her protection will have plenty of time to learn before I tear your throat out. I can hardly wait!"

The Adversary leaned down with one massive hand, and gently traced its claw over his cheek. Now, at last, Nuadhu did manage to scream.

Nuadhu's scream brought Anael sprinting from the outskirts of the village straight into Caiside and Genovefa's house. There, she found the boy sitting upright amidst a bundle of furs while his parents and younger brother looked at him, still groggy from having been shocked out of their own slumber. There was nobody else in the room.

"Are you okay?" She asked Nuadhu.

He nodded, looking ashamed. "I had a bad dream." He mumbled.

Of course he did, she thought. He's only ten, a child, and I'm teaching him to fight monsters. Even if it all seemed like a big adventure in the daytime, it would play on his mind in the darkness. How was it fair to place this burden on him?

She bent down and kissed him on the cheek. "You're safe." She told him. "And I'm on watch outside so nothing can get to you. Go back to sleep."

"What's the Great Adversary?" He asked.

She hesitated then. There was a look in his eyes that worried her. He saw something, in the dream. But if she told him now then he wouldn't sleep at all.

"I'll tell you in the morning." She said.

He looked doubtful, but his parents agreed eagerly, urging him to go back to sleep. He lay back down, but the haunted look didn't leave his eyes and his eyes never left Anael. She looked away, nodding to Caiside and Genovefa before turning and leaving the house.

Outside, several villagers were gathered outside their homes, and all turned to look at her as she left the house. Again, she thought back on Elisedd's warning about the feeling of some in the village regarding Nuadhu. How many were looking now thinking that this disturbance was only more proof that they would be better without her and the boy here?

"A child had a nightmare." She told them. "Nothing to worry about."

With some grumbling, they turned and went back to their beds. Only Elisedd didn't. He walked with Anael as she made her way back to the perimeter of the village.

"The Champion of Man screams in his sleep?" The chief said, his voice thick with cynicism.

"He's still a boy. You were never scared at his age?" She asked.

"Not of shadows."

"Well, of course not. You were never destined to protect people from the horrors that lurk in those shadows." With that, she stalked away to stand guard against the threat of Sons of Cain attacking the village in the night.

CHAPTER TWO

Several weeks after Anael had begun training Nuadhu and Pwyll, Judoc arrived in the town with a force of twenty warriors on horseback.

Although the warriors in Liuerpwl used lime to bleach and spike their hair in the traditional manner, in the town they were seen most often in normal clothing. Judoc's companions, on the other hand, were all topless and had their chests and faces patterned with blue woad. It was easy to see how fearsome a foe in battle or village suffering a raid might find these white haired, blue painted beasts, especially with their howling war cry.

There was no howling when they rode into the town, thankfully, but they caused enough of a stir despite that. Women hastily called children at play back to their houses, those on guard called for reinforcements, and farmers ran back from their fields to face the newcomers.

Nuadhu was among a group of children close to coming of age, fighting together using wooden swords, while Anael and Pwyll both watched. When she heard the thunder of hoof beats, she instructed them all to stay together and stay out of the way, before drawing her sword and running towards the commotion. The children's instructor knew better than to second guess her and herded them further away from the potential danger.

"Make way!" The front rider bellowed. "Make way for Judoc, son of Drustan, king of the Brigantes!"

At Judoc's name, Anael and the others with weapons drawn all raised them into the air. A cheer went up as the warriors rode past the salutes and, freed from the arms of worrying parents, children ran after the procession shouting and laughing.

Once the warriors dismounted, it was immediately clear who Judoc was. He stood a head taller than the tallest of his entourage, the torc at his neck gold where the others wore silver and while he was as bare chested as the others he had a cloak about his shoulders held in place by a golden brooch.

He was broad shouldered, thick necked, with a bushy red beard at odds with his white hair. His eyes were cold, no trace of human warmth in them, and one wider than the other so that he always looked as though he was glowering.

One of the other warriors drew in close to Judoc. He was perhaps fifteen, shorter and scrawnier than his father with only the threat of a beard, but the family resemblance was immediately apparent. Side by side they waited, until Elisedd presented himself and knelt before the king with his sword out in front of him.

Judoc bid Elisedd to rise with a gesture and then regarded the man for several moments. Finally, he slapped the chief's stomach and laughed. There was no humour in the sound. "I continue to be shocked that nobody has killed you in single combat for an easy promotion, old man."

Elisedd bore the insult stoically, while his people watched with clear embarrassment.

"How can I serve you, my king?" He said as though the jest at his expense had never happened. "We were not forewarned of your visit, so could make no preparations…"

Judoc waved away the apology. "Not to worry. My business here should be brief enough." He looked around at the assembled townspeople. "Where is the boy?"

Anael tensed.

"The boy?" Elisedd asked.

"Don't play the fool with me, Elisedd." Judoc said, raising his voice. "The boy. The one the demons of the Otherworld tried to claim ten years ago."

Anael cast about, to see if she could slip away unnoticed through the crowd to get to Nuadhu. But before she could move she saw him, moving with purpose towards the king, Pwyll trailing behind him. He stopped at Elisedd's side, dropped to his knees and presented his wooden sword to Judoc.

There was laughter all around, including from Judoc's warriors, but the king himself stayed stern and it died away quickly. He gestured for the boy to get to his feet and Nuadhu did, standing as tall as he could and puffing out his chest.

"Who are you, boy?" Judoc demanded.

"I am Nuadhu, son of Caiside, my king. I am the boy you are seeking."

Anael edged forward, mentally preparing herself to spring forward and fight off all the visiting warriors. Nobody noticed, as all eyes were on Nuadhu.

"Is that so?" Judoc looked briefly at Elisedd. "There is more iron in this boy than in you, Elisedd. Perhaps he ought to be the chief of Liuerpwl. Where are this boy's parents?"

Caiside and Genovefa both appeared out of the crowd, shuffling nervously. They took a knee and intoned "my king," reluctant to get too close to Judoc.

"Ah, not as bold as your boy, I see. Or as the boy hovering not too far behind him whom I presume from the likeness must be his younger brother. Tell me, is it true? Did the horrors that visited this town ten years ago come seeking your son?"

Caiside floundered, but Genovefa spoke up. "It is true, my king. They sought my son as I was giving him birth."

The king narrowed his eyes and ran a hand through his beard. "It is true then. I had feared as much." He nodded to his warriors, several of whom moved to put themselves between Nuadhu and his parents. "My sorrow will not make up for what I must do, but I offer you it nonetheless."

Many things happened at once. The warriors drew their weapons, making the townsfolk draw back. Some cried out in distress. Caiside and Genovefa tried to push forward, but found themselves gripped and held fast by the warriors facing them. Anael drew her sword. Judoc grabbed Nuadhu by the arm and drew a dagger, and when he realised what was happening Elisedd took hold of Pwyll to keep him back.

"Get off me!" Nuadhu shouted, struggling.

Judoc didn't respond, except to thrust the dagger at his heart.

Nuadhu shifted his weight and, with his free hand, punched at the weapon. His fist caught the flat of the blade and although the impact drew blood, it also bent and snapped the dagger. Judoc was taken aback enough by this to let go of the hilt.

Anael managed to force an opponent to the ground and then leap over him to get on the other side of the line of warriors.

"I see there is iron in your fists as well as your will!" Judoc snarled as he seized Nuadhu with both hands. "That will not spare you!"

Nuadhu continued to struggle and managed to catch Judoc in the jaw, sending him staggering backwards. Then Anael was at his side, her sword between the boy and the king. Nuadhu turned towards Elisedd, who panicked and shoved Pwyll towards him before fleeing.

Anael kept the brothers close behind her and stepped

away, as now all the warriors advanced upon her.

"Don't interfere with this, woman." Judoc said, stern but calm having composed himself once more. "That boy must die."

"You won't have him!" Anael said.

"No? Do you really think that this one town can hold off the full force of my kingdom – or even that they'll be willing to?"

Anael cast about. The townspeople were still staring, anxiety in their faces and their hands gripping their loved ones tightly. Everyone was scared. Caiside and Genovefa most of all.

Judoc followed her gaze. "Seize the parents!" He commanded. Two warriors grabbed them, forcing them forward to face Anael and their sons, then putting a sword to their throats. "Boy. Nuadhu, son of Caiside, I hold your parents' lives in my hand. With a nod from me they will die. Is that really the price you want to pay for your own miserable life?"

Anael managed to keep Nuadhu from charging forward, but it was a struggle. "Why do you want to kill me?" He shouted, the tears on his cheeks echoing in his voice.

"I don't want to kill you, boy." Judoc's tone softened, becoming almost sympathetic. "But as a king I must put the well-being of my whole kingdom before any one person, and if you live, we will all suffer the wrath of the Otherworld."

"That's not true!" Anael shouted. "Nuadhu is the only hope any of us have to survive the wrath of the Adversary!"

"What would you know of it, woman?"

In an instant Anael's wings were visible on her back and her whole body was glowing with golden light. "I know far more than you ever will, Judoc son of Drustan. Let the boy's parents go, leave this village and put your faith in the Champion as your only hope."

Judoc gave the slightest of nod. The two warriors holding Caiside and Genovefa pulled their heads back and cut. They screamed. The townspeople cried out, the splatter of blood snapping them from the trance fear had put them in. Nuadhu and Pwyll both roared with grief and anger.

Anael knew that the whole situation would be lost if she didn't act fast. She shoved the brothers hard, knocking them to the ground so that they couldn't attack in their grief and get themselves killed. Then she was sprinting at Judoc, and the warriors were drawing around their king to protect him. She could have cut through them all, but in that time she had no way to guarantee Nuadhu's safety. So instead she drew her knife and threw.

Then she was back with the brothers and picking them up in her arms before they could object. She flapped her wings, the beat rapid and deafening, creating its own wind. Once she was in the air, at least, they would be safe.

Once they were high enough in the sky, she took a moment to look down on the town. The death of Nuadhu and Pwyll's parents had spurred the people to take up arms against their king, and the song of iron rang out over ground quickly sodden with blood. Liuerpwl's warriors were standing their ground well enough with her training, but some of Judoc's force were on horseback once more, running down farmers, fishermen, mothers and children.

Judoc's men howled and whooped as they killed, all force and fury. It wouldn't be long until the fires started, and all that would remain of the town Anael had saved and helped defend would be the heads of its people, taken as prizes. She turned away, seeking out somewhere they could set down in relative safety.

They landed in a forest, miles to the south, beyond the reach of the river and with no human habitation within a day's walk. Once they were on the ground, Anael returned to a human form again. Pwyll was still crying, while Nuadhu roared and howled, kicking up clumps of grass and punching at trees, tearing up the bark but also bloodying his knuckles. Anael tried to stop him, to take hold of him and offer comfort but he pushed her away.

"I will kill him!" He shouted. "I will kill Judoc!"

"Nuadhu," Anael said as gently as she could, "Judoc has destroyed Liuerpwl and we won't be safe anywhere in Brigantia. We will need to stay on the move and go south whilst I continue your training."

"What good is my training if I can't avenge my parents?"

"If you don't train and fulfil your destiny, then your parents will have died in vain. You are the Champion of Man, and that means that you have a responsibility to fight the battles that nobody else can."

"Fine," Nuadhu punched the tree next to him one last time for good measure. "But I won't forget my parents. Judoc said that I have iron in my fists, and so I will take that as my name. It will be Nuadhu Iarraindorn who ends his life."

CHAPTER THREE

The next morning, the boys awoke to the smell of rabbit cooking on a spit, which Anael had snared just before dawn. After breaking their fast, they set off in a general southward direction on foot. After an hour or so of walking, Pwyll started to complain of headaches.

As the morning progressed, the complaints got worse. Several times, they had to stop and rest because he was clutching his head and screaming. There was nothing that Anael could do for him other than comfort him, and each time the pain eventually subsided to a dull ache, but as noon approached Pwyll was openly weeping as they walked.

"No I'm not!" He shouted suddenly, stopping and glaring at Nuadhu.

Nuadhu threw a confused look at Anael and then at his brother. "I didn't say anything."

"Yes you did! You said that I was acting just like a baby and you wished I would shut up!"

"No I never!"

"You did! I heard you!"

"I never! I..." A guilty look crossed his face and he lowered his voice. "I thought it. I never said anything though."

"I heard it!" Pwyll insisted.

"Pwyll, Nuadhu didn't say anything." Anael said, a thoughtful look on her face. "Can you hear anything now?"

"No. He's not saying – What? Of course I'm not imagining it!"

Anael looked at Nuadhu and raised her eyebrows.

"I did think that he was just imagining things." Nuadhu answered her look.

Pwyll looked up at her. "What does this mean?"

"Pwyll, I think you have the ability to hear people's thoughts." Anael said.

He shook his head. "No. Only the seer druids have that power. They have to train for years and fast in isolation while talking to the gods of the deeper forest before they can gain the ability to hear thoughts."

"Maybe that's how you train to have the power, but there are people who have a natural ability. It usually manifests in a time of intense emotions and great distress, which is what you've just suffered. Pwyll, I think you do have this power, you just haven't learned how to control it. That's why you've been getting headaches."

"What can I do about it?"

"Nothing yet. When we reach a town or village, we can find out where we might be able to find you someone to learn from."

"Oh, okay." Pwyll said, quietly, staring down at his feet. He looked lost, and the pain he was still enduring was written across his face. Tears continue to roll, but he never cried out, only moved past Anael and carried on walking.

Anael put a hand on his shoulder. "Pwyll are you…?"

He shrugged her off. "I'm fine."

Yet not half an hour later he was clutching his head again, not screaming this time but curled up on the ground and trembling. Nuadhu knelt next to him, shook his shoulder, and then looked up at Anael.

"What's wrong with him?"

"Hearing thoughts for the first time can be overwhelming experience. Many people need help to learn to control it, and I've heard of those who don't having to shut themselves away from other people to stop the pain."

"But there's only two of us here. Two people's thoughts can't be that bad."

"No…" Pwyll said through the pain. "Not just two… Everywhere."

"Don't be silly! It's just the three of us." Nuadhu looked around. "Could he be hearing animals' thoughts?"

"Maybe…" Anael said, though in truth she doubted it.

"Not animals…" Pwyll managed. "Dark…evil…"

Anael drew her sword and moved in a slow circle to scan their surroundings. But, like Nuadhu, she could see nothing. A squirrel dashed up a tree in the distance and birds sang in the canopy, but other than that she was certain that they were alone. At least, as far as normal senses could ascertain.

She shifted back to her archangelic form, the flap of her wings and the glow from her body sending several small animals fleeing from different hiding holes. She reached out into the forest with senses beyond those possessed by humans and mortal animals, feeling for…something.

What she found was dark and hot, feeding upon the light and energy around it like a parasite. Almost immediately she drew back from it, as though burned, and pulled back into human form. She looked up. It was high up in the trees, and now that she knew it was there she could see it, the faintest patch of grey among the greens, browns and blues of the trees and the sky. It was watching them.

Whilst Nuadhu still tended to his brother, Anael moved away several paces. The thing stayed where it was. She continued to watch it, then called for Nuadhu to lift Pwyll off the ground and come to her. When he did, supporting his brother with an arm about his shoulders so that he could walk despite still being in severe pain, the thing followed them.

"Wait here." She said.

Nuadhu looked alarmed. "Where are you going?"

"Ahead. To make sure it's safe. I won't be long."

He didn't look happy about it, but he stayed where he was while she ran ahead and found a likely spot. Nothing too conspicuous, but enough space that she could do what she needed to. Despite saying that she wouldn't be long, it was painstaking work to carve an exact shape in the ground whilst making sure that the grass was undisturbed enough that it couldn't be seen from above. When she was done, she made her way back.

Pwyll appeared to have recovered enough to walk of his own volition, but the pain of hearing the thing's thoughts was still writ large on his face. She looked up, and sure enough the grey spot still hovered high above them.

"Is it safe?" Nuadhu asked.

"It will be." She assured him. "Come on."

It was an effort not to have them simply sprint to the spot she had marked out. Instead, she maintained the pace that they had been walking at for the rest of the day, neither a march nor a stroll. Eventually, they came to it and Nuadhu and Pwyll walked through it without noticing it was there.

Then Pwyll screamed and fell to the ground. His scream was echoed by what sounded like the rumble of thunder given voice, high above. Sure enough, the emptiness was unable to move forward beyond the confines of her symbol. She took on archangelic form once more and touched it with her foot. A moment later it was visible to everyone, drawn in white light as well as carved dirt; only a circle filled with a star and certain sacred words of her native language, but enough to keep a demon confined while it was intact.

"Reveal yourself, demon. I, who bound you to this

place, command your appearance. Stand before me and answer to my summons. I command you. Reveal yourself!"

There was a flash of smoke and fire in the circle, and then it stood before them. It wasn't a particularly impressive creature; squat, flat-footed and grim, its night black skin marked with pocks and sores. Its head was spherical, topped by two short horns, with a wide mouth filled with needle-like teeth. There were two leathery wings on its back, a pointed tail at the base of its spine, and sharp claws on its hands and feet. A dirty, ragged tunic of human skin covered its nakedness.

Seeing Anael, it crouched as if ready to spring in attack and hissed at her. Pwyll stared at it with naked hatred, its thoughts still poisoning his mind. Nuadhu looked at it with more curiosity, and Anael had to gently hold him back when he approached the circle.

"What is that?" He asked.

"It's a demon." She said. "One of the Misbegotten – human souls tortured and broken down in Pandemonium until it is shaped into something else entirely. This."

"What's Pandemonium?"

"You might call it the underworld. It's where the Adversary who tried to kill you when you were born rules over demons and damned souls. They are the enemies of my people in Elysium." She addressed the demon, "Misbegotten, what is your purpose here?"

"I don't speak the tongue of your hairless apes, archangel." It said in the rasping, guttural language of its home realm.

"You were a hairless ape once yourself, abomination." She replied in the same tongue. "What is your purpose here?"

"It should be obvious enough. I was watching your boy."

"What is he saying?" Nuadhu asked.

"I'll tell you afterwards. Take your brother further on. His pain should subside away from the demon. Go on."

As Nuadhu went to help Pwyll up, she turned back to the Misbegotten. "Why were you watching him? Why is the Adversary so interested in this one?"

The demon only chuckled.

"Tell me!"

"Or what? You intend to kill me when this exchange is done, so what is my incentive to talk?"

"I can drag this out so that you beg for death otherwise, demon."

"Can you? I doubt it. You lack the tools, possibly also the will. And then there's the boy to think of. You can't just leave him to wander off in the forest alone."

Anael stepped forward and thrust her sword into the demon's abdomen. The howl this wrought from it sent birds flocking away in all directions. She twisted the weapon in the wound. The wail of agony grew so loud and so high that the ground shook around them. She pulled the sword out and the demon fell to its knees, panting and trembling. She offered it a questioning look.

"I will tell you one thing and one thing only." It said when it caught its breath. "You're going to lose, even if we don't kill your Champion. The war has already begun and he is far from ready to lead your side."

"What war is that?"

The demon chuckled again. "The last war. The war in which our father and king triumphs over yours, beginning with the complete subjugation of this world."

"That won't happen!"

"Won't it? Don't be so sure. All your certainty will be thrown in your face when these humans – all of them – are brought low, broken and twisted into things such as me."

"It won't happen. It won't."

"You sound almost certain." The Misbegotten offered her a grin filled with lust and hunger.

Anael let out a cry, all wordless anger and frustration, and swung her sword. The demon's head came off cleanly and its body fell lifeless to the floor. The light of the demon trap faded to leave burns in the grass under the carcass. She muttered curses, mostly at herself for letting the Misbegotten get the better of her and taunt her into a quick death.

When she caught up with Nuadhu and Pwyll, the younger brother appeared in a much better condition and the two of them were talking. They both looked back as they heard her approach.

"It's gone now." She told them.

"You killed it?" Pwyll asked. When she nodded, he said, "I thought so. The noise cut out so abruptly that I thought it must have died. As soon as it was gone the pain went and everything was so much easier. I can still hear Nuadhu's thoughts, but I think I can also shut them out."

"That's good. Keep practising that and it should help you to avoid any more headaches. When we get to a village, we can seek out a seer druid to teach you more about the powers you have while I continue to train Nuadhu."

"But I want to learn to be a warrior too! I might not have fists of iron or be a Champion of Man, but I can still fight!"

"Okay. But after what happened we're going to have to keep who you are a secret. We're out of Brigantes territory, so even revealing your tribe is dangerous enough. If the wrong people find out that Nuadhu is the Champion, it will put us all at risk. We need a different story, one that people will believe, but which hides who we truly are."

"We're a long way from any village yet, aren't we?" Nuadhu said. "We have a lot of time to think about our story. What we need right now is food." As if to support his assertion, his stomach growled.

CHAPTER FOUR

It took Anael, Pwyll and Nuadhu a little over two weeks to reach Wrikon, a hill fort that marked the heart of the Cornovii tribe's territory.

After exiting the forest, they first came upon a town called Dumniska which stood next to a particularly rich tin mine. They stayed there for several days, paying for their residence with the boys' labour in the mine and Anael's services fetching and carrying for a local smith. To the locals, she was a traveller from an island to the far west who had adopted the boys when she had found them stranded in a burnt-out village.

None of them were under the illusion that they could stay there long. It was too close to where the demon had pursued them, and the only druid in the town was an old drunkard whose wisdom had long since run dry. He claimed to know about reading thoughts, but when pressed on the matter had tripped over his own tongue and reached for a horn of ale for his salvation. Pwyll was for now able to hide his headaches, being nowhere as intense as when he had heard the thoughts of the demon, but they were getting worse.

Once they left Dumniska, Anael decided that they

ought to avoid other settlements until they reached somewhere they could find help. So they took a pack full of bread and several skins of water, from then moving through forestland, living off snared rabbits and squirrels. They took their time, never walking for the full day, and before it went dark Anael would have Nuadhu and Pwyll practising their swordsmanship with heavy branches.

Late in the night, Pwyll would wake up from nightmares and cry out for his dead parents. Nuadhu would come to comfort him and the two of them would share their tears and their grief. In the light of the day they never mentioned it, and appeared to all the world as though no ill had ever befallen them, so Anael followed their lead and acted as though she never heard them in the night.

Eventually, they reached Wrikon, and almost immediately Pwyll's headaches doubled him over.

Beyond a wall that stood thirty feet high and a deep earthen ditch, Wrikon rose from the ground in layers. What would have been a slow natural incline was carefully crafted into several steep drop-offs, with wooden stockades surrounding the town at the top. Before they even reached the bridge over the ditch to seek entrance, however, Pwyll was on the floor clutching his head as the sheer volume of thoughts washed over him like a wave.

The guards at the bridge wouldn't let them pass, insisting that Pwyll must have a sickness and they couldn't let it spread inside the walls. However they did confirm that there was a seer druid in Wrikon, in their words "the most powerful seer and wisest sage on the island of Britain," and agreed to send for him.

The druid's name was Guidgen. He was an old man, passing sixty, with a bent back and knobbled knees who struggled to walk even with a heavy oaken cane for support. He wore a black robe, turned grey with age, instead of the lighter robes traditionally favoured by his order. Almost entirely bald, he had a thick white beard which reached down to his stomach and a heavily weather lined face. But when he saw Pwyll and the pain he was in, he offered a kindly smile.

"This one suffers terribly." He noted, a not-too-helpful statement of the obvious.

Nonetheless, when he bid that Pwyll was stood upright and pressed his gnarled hands to the boy's temples, the result was instant. Pwyll fell silent and opened his eyes, blinking several times.

"What did you do?" Anael asked.

"I have placed a...barrier between Pwyll and the thoughts of others. It will remain there until I have taught him the skills to fully control his ability rather than be overwhelmed by it."

"How did you know his name?" Nuadhu said.

Guidgen smiled again. "The same way that I know you are Nuadhu and that your destiny will affect all of us. I have been a seer a long time, and though I do not wilfully intrude on the thoughts of others there is little which I need to know that can get past me. Like, for instance, the fact that if our king were to discover that you are here it would not bode well for anybody."

"Why not?" Anael put a hand to her sword, though her immediate thought was to run rather than to fight.

"Morcant is a good man," Guidgen said with a heavy sigh. "But dark words are flowing to us from the tribes over the water, to the east. They say that a great darkness is gathering, and that it will march our way because its enemy lives among us." He looked at Nuadhu. "You, child. The agents of that darkness put about that our death will stop the advance of the dark, and fearful men believe it. I see differently, that you are our Champion because without you we will all perish, but I am a minority and the king's mind will not be turned on this question."

"So what can we do?"

"Come with me. I am willing to help young Pwyll gain mastery of his powers, and to keep Nuadhu sheltered, because when you have skills such as mine it is hard to escape the realities facing us. But I cannot do it here." He turned and crossed one of the guard's palms with three silver coins. "I would have two horses brought here, so that I can ride out with my guests."

The guard was compliant enough, and soon enough the druid and Pwyll were on one horse and Anael and Nuadhu on the other. They rode out west of the hill fort until they came to a natural cave formation several miles away.

"These caves are perfect for solitude and contemplation." Guidgen explained. "They are where my master first taught me the mysteries of the mind and helped me hone my skills as a seer. I had many more years of it than you will, of course, Pwyll. But I am confident nonetheless that you will still excel at your study."

"We can't live out here, surely?" Anael said.

"Why not? I have adapted the place so that it has its comforts, such as straw beds, and I get my food fresh from the Wrikon markets. You will want for nothing, but you will also not be under the nose of a king who would likely fear to let you live if he discovered your presence."

"He had best not make the same mistake as Judoc." Nuadhu declared. "He killed my parents and I will have my vengeance upon him for that."

"I believe you, boy. But although I am here to help Pwyll and Anael is your teacher, please permit me to offer some wisdom. Revenge is a cure for nothing. It is poison, which will blacken your heart and taint your soul. Even if in the moment you feel vindication, afterwards what you did will haunt you."

"How would you know, old man?"

"I have lived a long life and experienced many things. I know."

Nuadhu regarded the druid mistrustfully, but Anael had already warmed to him. His tendency to give short answers at length, which would have otherwise been irritating, seemed endearing from him, and she believed that he genuinely wanted to help.

So they settled into the caves and, as Guidgen had suggested, they found it comfortable enough. By night, they slept on beds of straw inside the rock where with a small fire going the warmth settled like a blanket and the rhythmic sound of water running underground sent them easily into dreams. By day, Anael had Nuadhu and Pwyll training hard to become warriors.

The druid appeared infrequently. When he came, he would provide them ample supplies on which to survive, but also gifts. The two brothers gained swords and leather scabbards, whilst all three of them got new cloaks and ornate broaches to mark them out as being of high standing without suggesting they were of any particular tribe or allegiance.

Pwyll took to his own training, sporadic as it was, easily. Within a short period of time he had enough control of his ability that Guidgen thought he would be able to travel through a heavily populated town without the barrier that the druid had placed in his mind. After that, it was an easy enough leap to discover how to probe somebody's deeper thoughts, to school his own thoughts against other readers and to project his mind so that he could see through somebody else's eyes.

"I should be able to do that." Nuadhu commented once, after Pwyll had told him and Anael about what he was learning. "I'm the Champion of Man, so it makes sense for me to have that power."

"Nuadhu," Anael chided him, "you're strong beyond measure and a powerful warrior despite your young age. One day you will be a leader of men as well as their Champion. But others have their part to play as well, and Pwyll will have developed this power for a reason."

"I'm going to fight by your side and help you win." Pwyll insisted, puffing out his chest proudly.

Nuadhu only frowned, which in turn made Pwyll frown. He pushed his older brother.

"I am!" He insisted.

"You wish!" Nuadhu grabbed Pwyll's head and pushed him over, the two of them ending up wrestling on the ground.

Anael stepped forward to intervene, but then realised that they were giggling as they rolled around, and left them to it. In the midst of everything else that had happened to them and that was going to happen, she couldn't deny them this one moment to be children.

That opportunity would pass soon enough. They ended up staying in their new refuge for the next three years before the word came that they had to move on.

Nuadhu was now thirteen and just coming into manhood; his body shaped by the muscles forged of his training, his hair halfway down his back and his face lined with a faint fuzz that threatened to one day become a beard. Pwyll was still a child, now the age his older brother had been when they first arrived, but lean and athletic enough that you could see hints of the warrior he would grow into. They were sparring in the open with wooden swords when the rider came.

It was Guidgen's horse, but the rider was a girl somewhere between Nuadhu and Pwyll's age, the lack of any check and stripe pattern on her dress indicating that she was of low birth. She had thick red hair that hung to her waist in a loose braid and soft, pale features marked with freckles. As she rode towards them, Pwyll lowered his sword and stared open mouthed, so that Nuadhu struck him on the side of the head.

The girl pulled her horse up when Pwyll fell, a look of concern on her face. Anael had to put her hand to her mouth and suppress the urge to laugh, while Nuadhu made no such effort and ended up clutching his sides. After casting a baleful look in his direction, the girl dismounted and ran to Pwyll's side.

"Are you okay?" She asked, dropping to her knees and gently removing his hand from his head.

Pwyll looked up, the side of his head already bearing an impressive welt but only a hint of blood, and smiled. "I'll be fine." He said. "I'm… Hello. Who are you? I'm Pwyll. Are you okay?"

He was babbling, but it made the girl giggle. "I'm Caoimhé." She stood and helped him off the ground then looked over to Anael, his expression growing serious. "I'm a pupil of master Guidgen in Wrikon. He sent me to warn you, as he cannot come himself. You will have to leave."

"Leave?" Anael said. "Why?"

Caoimhé untied a heavy sack from the horse's back and pulled it down. "A man came to Wrikon to entreat king Morcant. My master says that there is something wrong with this man, a sickness, as though something unnatural and evil has taken residence inside of him."

"A demon." Anael cast a worried look at each of the boys in turn.

"It doesn't know where you are, master Guidgen says. But it believes that you are in Wrikon or close by, and it will convince Morcant that his life and the safety of his people depends on finding and killing you."

"Where can we go?" Nuadhu said. "Everywhere we run, these demons will turn people against us and see us hunted down."

"Master Guidgen says that you should go south. Cross the water and reach Gaul. The Roman Empire is not so easily intimidated by dark creatures, and there is an organisation there who will be able to help you, a guild."

"The Cycladic Guild of Warlocks." Anael said, the name returning to her easily despite it being several lifetimes since she last encountered them. "Yes, if they have influence with the empire, then we should be safe there."

"You can take the horse for your journey. My master has also sent supplies," Caoimhé gestured to the sack, "and also a gift." She reached into the sack and drew out a torc, heavy and ornately wrought with gold and silver spiralling around each other. "Nuadhu, Guidgen says that vengeance would only poison you, but purpose can give you strength.

"You must go south now, but he expects that you will return. When you do, your only hope will be in the unity of the tribes – a unity that only you can achieve by taking your place as their king."

Nuadhu took the torc, feeling the weight of it in his hands.

"Do not wear that openly until you unite the tribes. But when you do, it will be well suited well to a Champion of Man in his prime."

"You said you are Guidgen's student?" Anael asked.

"Yes."

"But you are a girl. Only men can become druids."

"Master Guidgen says that convention exists to be defied." She blushed. "He took me as a student for my natural ability to see the history of objects by touching them, but he says I have taken to other studies as though I was born to them as well."

"Maybe you should come with us then," Pwyll blurted out.

"I have to go back to Guidgen" Caoimhé said, blushing even more furiously.

"But…" Pwyll struggled for words, but found none.

Nuadhu came to his rescue. "Pwyll hasn't fully mastered his abilities yet. He needs someone to teach him, and even if you don't share his ability you must know enough about controlling powers that come from your mind to be able to help."

"She can't come with us, Pwyll." Anael said, aware even before she saw his reaction that she was crushing him. "She has a home and a life here."

"But that demon will find out that she helped us escape." Nuadhu said. "People will have seen her leave on Guidgen's horse and they'll see her come back without it."

Anael frowned, but Nuadhu was right. She looked at the girl, still unsure about any of this. "It's still your decision. If you think you should go back to your master…"

Caoimhé chewed her lip, then looked back at Pwyll again. "Master Guidgen did suggest that you might ask for my help, and he said it would be up to me if I thought it was the wiser course of action."

"What about your parents?"

The threat of tears glistened in her eyes then, and she quickly blinked them away. "They won't care," was all that she said on the matter. "But if Guidgen is hurt or threatened by the demon in his pursuit of Nuadhu…"

"Then there will be nothing you can do about it." Anael said, now aware that Caoimhé coming with them was all but a certainty. "It is better that you're not hurt or worse along with him."

So after returning the sack of supplies to the horse's back, and putting the torc back in it and out of sight, the four of them set off south.

It wouldn't be long before the demon brought King Morcant's forces down upon this place and laid it to waste, possibly other villages and even Wrikon itself as well. But they were not in a position to stop that even if they tried, and Nuadhu had to be kept safe until he could make a difference, so they fled.

Despite the dire situation, when they set off Anael noticed Pwyll continually sneaking glances at Caoimhé, and couldn't help but smile.

CHAPTER FIVE

They travelled south through another forest, dense with wildlife. After several days of walking, the group reached a village where Anael was able to trade some of their food, fresh deer and rabbit meat and a wolf pelt for the coin to purchase additional horses. After that, they rode hard to the south coast.

At a small, poor fishing village on the coast, they spent the horses in exchange for one of the two boats that were the village's only wealth. The village chieftain agreed to the exchange only when he was convinced that the horses were worth more than the boat and he was in fact robbing the travellers. Then he parted company with it easily enough and bid them farewell across the water.

The boat was tiny, fragile looking, barely big enough for the four of them. It was also unstable, rocking back and forth endlessly despite the relative calm of the waters as they set off. In truth, it was made for going out only short distances from the shore in order to cast nets and it would be a risk trying to reach Gaul in it. However, Anael judged it more of a risk paying for passage on one of the more regular crossing routes, so she took the oars and began to row.

It took half a day to get within sight of land on the other side of the crossing, and all three of Anael's wards strained to look. This was the furthest any of them had ever been from their homes, the first time that they had crossed an expanse of water, and they speculated about what wonders they might find on the other side.

"Guidgen told me about many mysteries and curiosities of the world," Caoimhé said. "He said that while our peoples know of the Otherworld, the sídhe and the children of Danu, there is much more beyond our borders that we could never dream of."

"Like dragons?" Pwyll said, with great enthusiasm. "My mother said that one of our elder druids told her about dragons. He said they were huge beasts with teeth as big as your head, scales and claws, and they can fly and breathe fire!"

"If they're so big and fearsome, why have we never seen them?" Nuadhu asked. "Why don't they run the world?"

"Because warriors fight them. That's why warriors dye their bodies with woad and spike their hair with lime and why they howl. It's so they look like the Sons of Mil and dragons know to fear them."

"There won't be dragons." Caoimhé said. "After they killed the lover of the hero Ninian, he tricked them by challenging them to a race from the Otherworld into our world. If they won, they could have his village and if he won they had to leave it alone. But once they were in the Otherworld they couldn't get back out, so now they're trapped there forever alongside Ninian."

"What will there be then?" Nuadhu asked.

"Romans, mostly."

"That's boring."

"No it's not." Pwyll insisted. "The Romans made pacts with gods and devils all over the world to build their empire, so that all kinds of monsters and magic call it home. Everywhere we go we'll be encountering strange things and we'll be having new adventures every day!"

Anael was too tired from the rowing to contribute to the conversation, but she smiled anyway. She knew enough of this world to put them right several times over, but sometimes it's more fun to speculate and then test your imaginings with experience. Instead, she focused on pulling the boat finally to the shoreline, where steady ground and rest beckoned.

Once they left the boat, it was only a short walk up the beach before the stone ramparts of a settlement became visible, archers walking along the top of it. They wore red tunics that reached to a little above their knees, covered by armour made of layered iron strips fastened together, iron greaves protecting their legs, and helmets with cheek and neck guards. Anael eyed them warily, but they glanced only fleetingly at the travellers coming in from the sea before once more going about their patrol.

Anael led them around the wall in search of a gate. When they found it, wooden doors standing open under a stone archway, they stopped to watch a line of slaves being led through.

All men, their skin ranging from pale as snow to deep black, their clothes rags that barely resembled whatever they might have once been, they were shackled one to the other and being led in a line. A black man at the front, powerfully muscled and dressed in a simple tunic, dragged them along. A white man in a cloak and trousers held a whip behind them, using it on those who slowed or stopped. Alongside the column, an elderly man in rich robes rode on horseback.

Once the column of slaves had passed, Anael led the way to the Roman soldiers at the gate. They glanced at her, sparing the longest look for the weapon at her hip, and then bid her enter.

"What town is this?" She asked, in Latin.

"Augustodurum." The soldier said, sounding bored and irritated.

Anael thanked him and then led Nuadhu, Pwyll and Caoimhé inside.

Within the walls, there were few stone structures. A spa, a bathhouse and a small amphitheatre were all clearly visible, but they stood alongside roundhouses built of mud, straw and wood, while the main street was lined with wooden market stalls. The air was thick with the stench and sound of people and animals, though the sky was growing subtly darker as the day wore on towards its end.

"I'll have to teach you to speak Latin if we're to be here a while." Anael told them. "We need to contact the Guild, and find out as much as we can about what the Adversary's plans are, as well as continuing with your training. But first, we need to find somewhere we can get clean and rested."

There was an inn next to the bathhouse. After purchasing rooms for them to sleep in, Anael took them to the bathhouse where immersion in a cold pool, sweating in a warm room and then immersion in a hot pool cleaned them of the dirt and fatigue of their long trip over land and water. A meal of roasted duck, hard bread and stewed vegetables in the inn followed, leading them all into a deep sleep.

On the next morning, Anael went out to make inquiries about the Guild. Not knowing where to begin, she sought out the town magistrate, who was called Bricius and would often hold audiences and hear petitions from the townsfolk in his long-hall. He wasn't to be found there, however, and she came upon him in the square at the centre of the main street talking with another town official.

Both wore long silk togas in the Roman senatorial style, but with torcs around their necks. The magistrate's torc was gold, indicating that if Gaul weren't part of the empire he might have been a chieftain, while the thick open ring around the other official's neck was silver. The magistrate was a relatively young man, athletically built under his rich clothing, while the other official was a thick set old man.

"Magistrate," she called to him, "pardon my intrusion, please, but I require to speak with you on an urgent matter."

Bricius gave her a lustful smile that set her on edge, then turned and nodded a dismissal to the official. "Yes, my dear." He said, reaching out a hand and stroking her arm. "I am always happy to help those who seek me out."

She smiled back at him even as her skin crawled, resisting the urge to flinch away from him or to lash out.

"Pray tell," he went on, "from where do you hail? As you have no doubt seen for yourself, my fair town is blessed with visitors from across the known world, and yet I must say that I have never encountered anybody as…enchanting as you." He leaned in close, his breath hot and sour against her face. "You must come from the realm of the gods, surely?"

That drew a genuine smile, just for a moment, at the unintentional accuracy of Bricius's absurd attempts at flattery. She swallowed it and petitioned him as though she hadn't just endured his leering. "Magistrate, I will be blunt. I am wondering if you know of an organisation called the Cycladic Guild of Warlocks, or perhaps simply The Guild?"

He drew his hand back then and frowned at her. He lowered his voice to a harsh whisper. "Who are you? What do you want with the Warlock Guild?"

"You know of it?"

"I know many things, but not who you are, woman."

She found the sudden sharpness in his tone easier to deal with than his previous over-familiarity. "My name is Anael. I was told that the Guild may be of some help in a matter that I have to deal with."

The magistrate regarded her even more distrustfully now. "I have no reason or compulsion to trust you, woman. But I must get to the bottom of the matter of how you know of the Guild." He glanced around him, then clicked his fingers. Several Roman soldiers appeared around them, as if from the shadows. "Will you follow me willingly or must I have the soldiers seize you?"

She chose to follow the magistrate on her own feet, rather than be dragged. She could only hope that Nuadhu, Pwyll and Caoimhé would heed her instructions and not leave the inn until she returned.

They went into the amphitheatre, going not up into the tiered stone seating but down onto the dirt-filled open space in the middle. Bricius led the way down the tunnel and through various chambers built underneath the main structure. Most held cages, either for slaves or for animals, and Anael recognised the slaves who had been brought into the town the day before among those held. But the end room was bare and empty.

"We can speak plainly in here, I think." He said. "Anael, I want you to tell me precisely what business you claim to have with the Warlock Guild. Only if I know the full truth can I help you, as you have asked."

"Why should I trust you? You have taken me far away from witnesses and surrounded me with armed men."

"Yet I have let you keep your own weapon." He pointed out. "My motives here are not malevolent, merely diligent."

She shrugged, realising that she had no choice unless she wished for a bloodbath. "Very well. I am here because very dark forces are amassing that threaten us all, and I am hoping that the Guild will be able to help me discover what these dark forces are trying to do and how to stop them."

"Interesting." Bricius said. "What kind of dark forces?"

"I don't know. But I do know that the creator of all demons is abroad on the earth for the first time in millennia and that whatever is happening is at his command."

There were several moments of silence before Bricius nodded. The soldiers around her stepped back from her to stand in formation, then the magistrate turned away from her and faced the wall. He muttered some words which Anael couldn't make out but which she recognised as Greek from the inflection. Then there was a click and a section of the wall slid backwards and scraped open as if on a hinge.

"I apologise for the interrogation, Anael." He said. "But we had to be absolutely sure that it was you before we brought you in."

He led her through the doorway, and down and spiralling stone stairwell illuminated by flaming torches held in sconces on the wall. As they descended, leaving the soldiers behind, the door scraped closed behind them.

At the bottom of the stairwell lay a broad, dark room, dimly lit by fires in the four corners. Shelves filled with scrolls, books and manuscripts lined the walls on either side while a single large table dominated the centre of the room.

"I don't understand." She said.

"The seer druid Guidgen sent you our way. He was a good friend to the Guild in a time of crisis not so long ago and we have maintained a correspondence. He sent a pigeon to us bearing a message that you would be coming with the Champion of Man and that we had to help you discover what dark future lay ahead of us."

"You're a warlock of the Guild then?"

"Me? No. I never had an aptitude for magic, but I dare say that the Guild has expanded considerably since your last encounter. It is no longer a Guild in the strictest sense, the combination of the world's most powerful warlocks for a common interest. Each of them now commands divisions with a much wider remit, policing the interaction of the human world with the supernatural. Or at least, as much of the human world as we can expand our influence to."

"Which is mainly the Roman empire, from what I have heard. What does this policing involve?"

"Exactly what you might expect. The slaying of

monsters, the exorcism of demons, and so on. Our activities are quite extensive."

"Do you know what's going on, then? What we're up against?"

"I am afraid not. As you say, our influence only stretches to the borders of the empire, and whatever the Great Adversary is up to he is doing it beyond. Most likely in the barbarian territories of the north east of Europe. We can help you find out, however, while providing you with somewhere that the Champion can train and grow in relative safety."

Anael hesitated to offer an answer.

"You are still wary of accepting our help." Bricius said.

"I still know next to nothing about you, and this all feels...too easy."

He moved as if to put his hand on her arm again, though this time consciously stopped himself. "You are wise to not offer your trust too readily, but I can assure you beautiful one," the phrase gave her a feeling akin to insects swarming over her skin, "that we are very much on the same side."

Anael shrugged him off. "Convince me."

"Very well." He nodded his head. "Follow me."

He moved around the table to the far end of the room from where they had come in. There, he pressed a latch and opened a door that she hadn't even seen before. At his beckoning, she followed him through into a room even colder and darker than the one that they were in.

This one was a dungeon, without a doubt. An enormous iron grille, the door in the middle of it locked, blocked off three quarters of the room. On the other side, through heavy black shadows, she could just about make out the shape of a man chained to the wall, his body slumped against the floor.

"Anael, meet Bricius, the magistrate of Augustodurum."

She put a hand to the hilt of her sword. Bricius, or the

man pretending to be Bricius as seemed to be the case, saw her do so but reacted only with a thin smile.

"This is the man who you would have approached regarding the Guild had we not received the message from Guidgen." He stepped forward and unlocked the door. "Come and see for yourself."

She stepped into the doorway. A moment later, with the rattling of chains, the man leapt up and ran at her. His shackles held him a foot away from her, but it was close enough even in the darkness to see him for what he was. His skin was a rotten yellow-grey, with red eyes, sunken cheeks, and a mouth filled with sharp, needle-like teeth. He thrashed and growled, lashing out with clawed hands though he was too far away to land a blow.

"He's one of the Sons of Cain." She said.

"Yes. One of several blood drinking revenants that the Adversary had placed to intercept you should you try to cross the water from Britain. We believe that we have gotten all of them."

"And are they all chained up like this?"

"We thought that you might like to see proof that we shared the same interests."

"Okay. And what about you? You appear to have no trouble being accepted as the magistrate of Augustodurum."

"A simple enough glamour. Or at least I am assured so, as I have said, magic is not a skill I can lay claim to. Between that and the man's...over-familiar manner..." he shuddered, as though he was as repulsed by this as she had felt earlier, "and my identity is unquestioned."

There seemed to be nothing else that she could say. "Very well, I'll accept your help to find out what threat the Champion is facing."

"Excellent. Though there is one matter to attend to first."

He gestured to her sword. She didn't need telling twice, and in one sharp motion her weapon was drawn and the head of the shackled, undead Bricius was separated from the body.

CHAPTER SIX

At sixteen, Nuadhu stood over six feet tall, heavily muscled, with thick ruddy-brown hair past his shoulders and bristly facial hair. He was now a formidable fighter, as well as being able to speak several languages and well versed in the lore of demons, the Sons of Cain and other creatures he might be expected to face.

Despite this, he remained almost entirely unknown, since Anael had been so insistent upon keeping him hidden from potential threats until he was ready. He had insisted more than once that he was ready, but this had fallen upon deaf ears and so he remained stuck in Augustodurum with only Pwyll and Caoimhé for company. Though he often felt as though he was intruding given that he couldn't relate to their shared interest in the powers of the mind. Too often, he would be simply and observer to their conversations, and usually able to slip away without either noticing or passing comment.

He got on well enough with Anael, but her over-protectiveness of him was infuriating.

"Do you remember what I asked you on the very first day that we trained together," he asked her one day as they sparred in a clearing outside of the town, "back in

Liuerpwl?"

"About me having wings?" A frown creased her brow as she thought back.

"No. About what your father wanted you to be."

"Oh, that." She smiled. "That was a very long time ago, well remembered. But why?"

"I asked you because you were saying that Pwyll should follow our father's wishes and become a farmer. But you never answered me."

"What does it matter? He never had to take up farming."

"No. But I've struck enough clean blows on you in the intervening six years that you probably owe me a few answers."

"I didn't realise we were still playing that game."

He grinned. "You never said that we had stopped."

"So?"

"So tell me. Tell me about your father and what he wanted for you."

Their voices fell away, leaving only the continued song of blade upon blade as they thrust and parried, moving about in a well-practised rhythm.

"My father is called Michael." Anael said eventually. "He is the head of the archangels, general of the forces of Elysium and second in command to our Creator, the Father of all of us."

Another pause punctuated by the clash of swords.

"But my mother was an archangelic warrior too. Her name was Sidriel, and not too long after my birth she was killed defending Elysium from an attack by archdemons. However, from then my father was adamant that I wouldn't become a warrior as he didn't want to lose me in the same way."

"So he was over-protective?"

"Is that what you think I am?"

"I'm the Champion of Man, there's no way to avoid me being a warrior and being put into harm's way."

"No, but there's no need to actively rush you into danger."

"Why are you so worried about me?"

"Because it's my job to protect you."

"It's your job to train me."

"And to keep you safe."

"Not to keep me from living, though."

The clash of swords became more frequent and more frantic, each step hastier and each swing harder. They were both sweating as they moved in quick circles, only inches apart, both on the offensive.

"I'm trying to keep you alive!"

"You think I'd die if I had a real taste of the things I'm supposed to fight?"

"If you're not ready, yes!"

"I am ready!"

"Are you?"

Nuadhu spun away from Anael, dodging her next thrust. He kicked out her legs and jumped on top of her, pinning her arm down and putting his sword to her throat. For just a moment, he saw fear in her eyes, at the same time as he realised that they were the deep green of emeralds. He loosened his grip, his arm shaking and his breathing rapid and heavy.

Anael was also panting, her mouth open in shock and her eyes following his. She reached a hand up and touched his arm, bringing up goosebumps and making his hairs stand on end.

"Nuadhu..." She said his name almost as a whisper.

"Anael...?" He felt a stupid grin spreading across his face.

She pushed up off the ground, gripping his sides with her legs and rolling backwards. The movement took him completely by surprise and he ended up on his back with her blade now at his throat.

"You're not ready yet."

She stood up and sheathed her sword, then looked

down at Nuadhu and offered him a hand. He stared up at her, trying to hold on to his anger, but instead found himself looking at Anael in a way that he never had before. His chest felt tight and his stomach was fluttering.

"Nuadhu? Are you okay?"

He pushed himself to his feet and stormed off, his cheeks burning.

Rather than go back into the town, he went further into the forest, his thoughts and emotions all a-tumble. Each time he felt as though he had hold of one tangible train of thought, something else would force it aside. He wanted Anael to realise that he was fully capable of looking after himself and to give him some responsibility so he could grow into his role as Champion of Man. But then he remembered the feeling as her hand touched his arm, the closeness of their bodies on the ground, and something other than anger stirred inside him.

He kicked at a nearby tree, then slumped against it. He took several deep breaths and managed to calm himself down, but not to order his thoughts.

Anael found him ten minutes later, still sitting in the same position on the floor. He glanced up as he heard her approach, and felt himself blushing again. She offered him a sympathetic smile.

"I know that you're more than capable of taking care of yourself." She said. "But we don't know what we're getting into yet, and the Adversary isn't a threat that you treat lightly."

Nuadhu forced himself into a standing position. "I'm not. But you don't defeat an enemy by running and hiding from them. You haven't even been able to find out what the Adversary is up to, so how can we ever defeat him?"

"We're trying to find out, me and the Guild."

"But how? The answer is out there beyond the borders of the Empire, not in an ancient scroll written in a dead language."

"No, you're right. But I haven't been looking in the

Guild's archives to find out what is happening in the east. I've been looking trying to find out how we might defeat the Adversary."

"Most dark creatures can be killed either by removing their head or by removing their heart."

"Yes, but the Adversary is not most dark creatures, he is their creator. He built the underworld and has stood fast against entire choirs of angels. He isn't simply another monster to be slain in some careless attack."

Nuadhu felt his anger rising again, for the moment brushing away all other feelings. "Then where are the armies of Elysium to fight him? Why is your father or your Creator not leading the assault? This task has fallen to me, and I have never shied away from my own destiny, but you have to give me the chance to fulfil it."

"Nuadhu…" She reached out to him and he flinched away, though some part of him didn't want to. "Your destiny isn't simply to be sent out against an unknown threat to fight and die. Like your forebears as Champion, you are the person best suited to lead mankind against the threat facing them, to help them stand firm against it, and to give them victory. I believe in you. But you are not invulnerable. Nobody is."

He could see the worry written large on her face, and knew that it was genuine. He took a deep breath to steady himself, forcing his anger down and stretching out his fingers at his side to avoid clenching them into fists.

"Okay." He said, choosing his words carefully. "I realise that we cannot just charge blind into this fight. But let me help you, at the very least I might be of some use figuring out what it is we are up against."

"Well, as you say there isn't much that ancient scrolls can tell us. The Guild have detailed records of the many different challenges that they have faced, and records of more preternatural creatures from the known world than even I have encountered. But nothing on the Adversary or how we might fight him. So all we can do is find out what he is doing."

Nuadhu thought he had misheard that. "We?"

"Yes. You are right, you are of age now and your skills need to be tested. Just be aware that we will be travelling to find out what the Adversary is doing, we will have to regroup before we actually face him."

He nodded, perhaps too quickly, simply eager to be underway now that Anael had finally decided to entrust him with a mission.

"Where are we going?" He asked. "Besides 'east'?"

"We don't know." She said with a shake of her head. "What we do know is that over the past few years it has been reported that the tribes of Germania have been moving west, towards the borders of the Empire. The Roman General Germanicus is leading a campaign against the chieftain Arminius out there, so the Romans are assuming that these new arrivals are reinforcements."

"But they're fleeing from something."

"Yes. Whatever the Adversary is doing appears to be expanding westward, and as it does the tribes are shifting their settlements to get away from it. But of course that leads them right into the battle between Arminius and Rome."

"How soon before we can head out to discover what is forcing them westward?"

"Within days, I would imagine. Now, shall we head back into town?"

He nodded and followed her back out of the forest towards Augustodurum. As they walked, he tried to find something to say, but found it near impossible to make small talk. He kept throwing furtive glances at her and then hastily looking away, fearing she would see him starting at her.

Eventually, she asked him, "Are you okay?"

"Yes." He said, too quickly. "Why?"

She shrugged. "You're very quiet."

"Oh, I'm just a little tired."

"You'll need to make sure you're well rested before we leave. In truth, I'm quite looking forward to it."

"You are?"

"Yes. It's a break from routine, and I feel as though I've spent the last three years buried in scrolls and manuscripts."

Within a couple of days, they had a pair of sturdy young horses and ample supplies for the first leg of their journey. They bid farewell to Pwyll and Caoimhé, who would continue to stay at the inn and practice their skills under the protection of the Guild, and set off at dawn in the late spring.

It would take them a little over a week to reach the edge of the Roman Empire, where its forces were about to collide with those of the Germanic tribes. But that would be the easy part of the journey, before they crossed into unfamiliar territory to seek out a danger they yet knew nothing about.

CHAPTER SEVEN

Amassed and in rigid formation, the Roman legions presented a fearsome sight. A sea of red, marked by the standard of each legion, the tunics and cloaks the soldiers wore and by the shields, moving in harmony like one organic body. A body whose function was to deliver death and conquest.

Everybody had their positions; infantry at the front, cavalry to either side of them, archers behind on higher ground, stakes and ditches marking out the Empire's positions. Their armour was dull and dirty, but still visible as a reminder that it would not be so easy for the enemy to run a blade through them.

By contrast, the Germanic tribes were a disordered mass. Dressed in thick furs, with long hair and heavy beards, they were spread out in a loose line. They waved their weapons, axes and swords mostly, in the air and hollered threats and boasts in the direction of their foe. They had some cavalry, but not many, and no shields or archers. If Nuadhu had to make a guess, he would say that the tribesmen would lose.

However, Nuadhu was not here for the battle. The war horns sounded in earnest, drowning out the bellowing of the tribesmen, and a line of oil was set alight in front of the archers for them to dip their arrows in. As they shot a trail of fire across the open field, Nuadhu and Anael urged their horses into a trot and kept to the trees as they made their way past the battle.

"They're only defending what's theirs." Nuadhu observed, as he glanced over at the battle. "If the Romans ever came for the Brigantes, we would be ready to fight just like the people of Germania."

"This isn't our concern." Anael reminded him.

"You cannot be uncaring about what the Empire is doing abroad."

"I do care, and the injustices of this world extend far beyond the expansion of territory through military conquest. But we can't change how men behave towards one another; we can make sure that they survive much greater threats long enough to change their own ways."

The battle raged on, the air thick with the smell of killing and the ground slick with mud churned up by thousands of feet. In between, iron and flesh collided to draw more blood. Men and horses alike roared and screamed as adrenaline or dread and pain overtook them.

"Let's get going, then, if we can't intervene." Nuadhu said.

They spent the next three weeks riding east. They avoided settlements as far as possible, making camp in the forest and eating only what they could forage, hunt or catch in traps. Although they had plentiful supplies of bread and salted meat, Anael insisted that they save this in case whatever the Adversary was doing meant that they couldn't hunt or forage when they got close to it.

Although they avoided settlements, it was near impossible to avoid people. Soon enough, they found a well-travelled trail running east to west, and as they rode in the opposite direction they came across great numbers of people travelling it. Sometimes in long caravans, horses and crude carts laden with supplies, other times in ones and twos with only the clothes on their backs.

Nuadhu and Anael had dressed simply, in cloaks lined with wolf fur, tunics, trousers and hide boots, so that there was no look of the Empire about them. They spoke to the refugees in their own tongues. On several occasions they offered to share freshly caught meat because those they passed looked starved. Yet all they ever got was silence and suspicious looks, for the fact that they were travelling towards what these people were fleeing.

Eventually, the trail of people dried up and they didn't have to avoid the settlements because they were deserted. Usually, they were picked clean of everything of worth, only the immovable structures of mud and timber left intact. But they offered a roof over the head and warmth, so Nuadhu and Anael took shelter when they came across it.

A week after they discovered their first empty village, the trail they had been following started thinning out, indicating that fewer people had come from this far east. Ahead of the next village they came to heavy stakes planted in the ground with rotting wild boar heads atop them and a wooden sign between them, bearing only an 'x' smeared in blood. Inside the village, they discovered three hastily dug graves.

As they travelled on, they found more warning signs marked by boar heads and smeared blood. The trail continued to thin out, while the number of graves expanded. Soon enough, they came to a village where the dead weren't even buried, but still they had been given treatment that must have been doled out also to those put underground; their heads had been cleaved from their bodies and stakes had been planted through their chests.

"They feared that their dead would rise." Nuadhu said. "But as what?"

"Look at their wounds," Anael said, pointing to the tears across the necks of the corpses, made by sharp teeth. "This is the work of the Sons of Cain."

Beyond this village, the trail disappeared altogether. However, they noticed a shape looming beyond the forest to the south east. They tied up the horses and entered the forest on foot. The sky was beginning to darken, but they were so close now that they decided to press on.

The forest was thick and dark, no light passing through the canopy and the floor crunching underfoot. There were no other sounds, however, suggesting that there was no wildlife at all in the vicinity. They pushed through blind, the darkness crushing and the heat rising as branches and thorns tried to slow their progress.

Eventually, they forced their way into a clearing and found themselves in the shadow of an enormous stone fort. The structure rose out of the hillside, the ramparts framed by turrets and surrounding a great, grey walled keep. It was incomplete, however, with considerable gaps in the stonework of the keep in particular.

"What is this place?" Nuadhu whispered. "Even the Romans don't have forts like this."

"Look." Anael pointed up at the battlements, where figures patrolled back and forth in shadow. "What do you see?"

Something about the figures prickled at Nuadhu's senses. He couldn't quantify it, but immediately he got the sense that they weren't human. "Sons of Cain?" He asked her, as a guess.

"Most likely, given what we saw in the village. But it appears that they're acting as soldiers rather than merely lone hunters. If only we knew to what end..."

"That's what we're here to find out."

Anael put a hand on his chest. "Yes, but without putting ourselves at risk. Come on, we'll be able to see more at first light."

Nuadhu didn't look happy about it, but he nodded in agreement. So they made their way back to the horses and led them inside the village. Anael argued that it was unlikely anybody would return there and so the animals were less likely to be spotted.

Neither of them were able to get any sleep in those few hours, and after each took their turn laying on the ground and staring into nothingness, the sun started to come up. The light still didn't penetrate far into the forest, but it still made their travel to the fortress marginally easier. They arrived there to the sounds of activity.

The Sons of Cain still walked the battlements, their sunken cheeks, grey skin and red eyes clearly visible under the glare of the morning sun. They had long hair and thick beards covering their dead faces, which along with the furs they wore suggested that in life they had come from the Germanic tribes. However, over the fur they wore plate armour covering their torso and forearms.

Beyond them, they could see now that where the keep was not yet complete wooden scaffolds had been raised against it and a winch carried fresh stones up while the sound of masonry work was clear enough. Looking at the small shape of the stone workers, Nuadhu again got the sense that they were not human. However he also knew, and again he couldn't put his finger on any tangible reason that he might know this, that they were a different kind of not human than those patrolling the walls.

One of them stood up, his motions awkward and unsure, and instantly Nuadhu knew what they were. He wore thin, mouldy rags over a grey body, with a thin, frail looking face, sunken eyes and lips drawn back from the gums. In short, the stone mason was a corpse.

"This fort is being built by the dead. Your Adversary must keep company with necromancers."

"He doesn't need to," Anael said. "He has a power over corpses that a sorcerer playing with death couldn't hope to match. He gave Cain the power to kill and have his victims come back as his Sons. Having revenants build him a fort would be nothing next to that."

"Yes, but why?"

A short while later, their answer came with the thunder

of hooves. The beasts were draped in plate armour when they came into sight, the metal covering their sides and their underbellies. There were maybe a hundred of them, their riders all Sons of Cain. Half were like the guards on the walls, Germanic with armour over their furs. The other half wore pointed hoods, long fur-lined jackets and trousers decorated in multi-coloured patterns with boots tied at the ankle. They had the same armour over this, yet the outfit marked them out as coming from further east, beyond Germania.

Trailing behind the horses were enough people to populate an entire village, men, women and children, connected and drawn by shackles around their necks. All of them were barefoot and ragged, the children's faces lined with snot and tears, the women's clothes torn open. Some of the shackles contained corpses, by the looks of it people who had failed to keep pace and for that failure been strangled by their chains and had their body shredded by the road. Most of the dead were elderly or children.

Nuadhu tensed up and again Anael put a hand on his chest, mouthing 'we can't.' Logically, he knew that she was right but still adrenaline surged through his body. It didn't feel right to stand here, hidden, while these people suffered.

The iron portcullis that was the entrance to the fort raised up, most likely drawn by a winch, and three dead men came through. The leader of the horsemen dismounted and walked to them, shouting and pointing in a language Nuadhu couldn't speak. He understood the implications well enough, though, as the corpses started unshackling the terrified villagers and herding them into two groups.

The purpose of these groups was easy enough to guess with their make-up. The first was made almost exclusively of adult men, though there were a couple of strong looking women among them. These, Nuadhu reasoned, were to be turned into Sons of Cain.

The dead were also unshackled and carried to the second group. With them, everyone who had not been picked for the first group. Women, children, the weaker of the men. Being put with those who had fallen on the journey to the fort was a clear enough message, which even the children got as it sent them into tears and hysterics; they were to die. Some, Nuadhu guessed, would be brought back to serve the Sons of Cain in some way. The rest would be no more than their food, drained of their blood and cast aside.

Once they were all lined up, the walking corpses herded them inside the fort. Then the riders followed and the portcullis was brought down behind them.

"We have to save them." He whispered to Anael.

"We cannot," she answered. "We are too vastly outnumbered. We would die, they would still die, and many more would suffer the same fate."

"So instead we run?"

"We sound the alarm, let people know what is coming so that they can prepare for it. Then you must fulfil your destiny, to unite the tribes against this threat."

"How long will all of this take? We can end this now!"

"No we can't! Don't you see? The Adversary's plan is not simply a fort for the Sons of Cain to use as a base when hunting."

Realisation hit Nuadhu hard, draining the anger and horror that had been spurring him on to charge straight in. "This is not the only fort, and these are not the only Sons of Cain raiding villages for food and recruits."

"Exactly." Anael said. "They are expanding slowly, but they are expanding – east and west. The Sons of Cain are creating an army, and with them the Adversary intends to conquer all of humanity."

CHAPTER EIGHT

On the return journey, Nuadhu and Anael discovered that there had been more Germanic migration westward and more villages left abandoned. After a week and a half of riding and the last empty village, they came upon a series of fortifications stretching to the north and south which marked a border and barricade against the foe that they had fled.

There were a series of earthen ditches, each separated by arrangements of sharpened wooden stakes which would have been nearly impossible to climb. Beyond them, wooden ramparts whose guards were armed with heavy war axes.

"We won't be able to get across on horseback." Nuadhu said. "If at all."

"No," Anael agreed, "And we can't afford the detour north or south to find a gap either."

They dismounted the horses and unburdened the animals of their supplies, before urging them away southward to find their own way. The animals hadn't complained at all on the journey, but must have had a sense of what lay behind them as they didn't need much encouragement to set off at a gallop.

Anael took on archangelic form again, spreading her wings. "I don't like drawing this much attention to myself, as a rule. We'll find somewhere hidden on the other side of these barricades to land, and then we'll need to acquire more horses to be on our way."

Nuadhu didn't argue. He stepped into Anael's arms when bidden, ignoring the acrobatics his stomach did at their embrace, and let himself be carried into the air.

He could barely remember the last time that this had happened, as a child when Judoc had laid waste to his town. Now, it felt dizzying and made his head swim as the world spun around him. They moved so fast, under the furious beating of Anael's wings, that he had no time to take in much of what he saw. Before he knew it, they were landing again, hidden in a thick copse, and as Anael resumed human form Nuadhu's legs struggled to steady him.

They came to the next village, a brand-new construction built by those who had fled from much farther east, as refugees. Inside, the villagers offered them a warm enough welcome and they were granted an audience with their chieftain.

The new chieftain was a young man called Gustaf, recently ascended to the position after the death of his father. He was tall and strong, but unsure of himself in a leadership role. He received Nuadhu and Anael as strangers without a tribe, since they had decided not to try and explain their true identities.

"We have never seen anything like this before." He told them, in Germanic. "Strigoi, yes. But they rarely stray from the mountains and are restricted to the darkness. They move exactly as you would expect the dead to, stiff and clumsy. They are easily dealt with. But these creatures are something else.

"Sunlight is no restraint upon them. They are strong, agile, organised in a way that strigoi are not. We have no name for them as we have never encountered them before, and yet now they send us fleeing like goats from a wolf."

"My people call them the Sons of Cain." Anael said.

"You know of them, then?"

"Yes, too well. Usually, they hunt alone or in small groups who shared a nest. They kill only when hungry, and very rarely turn a victim into their kind. The ritual to do that involves not only drinking the victim's blood but also letting them drink their sire's blood in return. You need to remove their head to kill them."

"This knowledge will be useful to my people. But if they usually exhibit different behaviours, why are they acting like this now?"

"We believe that they are acting under the command of a higher power, the dark thing that created them. Its name is Ahriman, though my people usually refer to it as the Adversary. It is more powerful than any other force on this earth, and it is turning the Sons of Cain into an army whose aim is to conquer man."

Gustaf paled at this, shifting in his seat. "You are certain of this?"

Anael nodded.

"Then what can we do?"

"What you are doing now is the right course of action. Your tribes need to be united against this foe, and you need to defend against their coming in any way that you can."

"There is to be a meeting of chieftains to discuss this threat. I will tell them everything that you have told me and urge this course of action. Perhaps you can attend as my advisers?"

Now Anael shook her head. "We cannot do that. We must travel west, as we have our own duties to fulfil to ensure that we can see off this enemy."

"You would leave me to convince the chieftains alone?"

"You are a chieftain yourself and you have seen the threat first-hand. You can convince them."

Gustaf seemed extremely unsure of this prospect, but he nodded anyway. "I will try."

Anael stood up and touched his hand as an act of reassurance. Nuadhu felt irrationally jealous of the chieftain in that moment. "May the gods smile upon your efforts."

After their audience, though he still looked reluctant to see them go for the prospect of having to pass on the information Anael had given him by himself, Gustaf provided them with two horses so that they could ride west.

The Romans had defeated the Germanic tribes in the battle that Nuadhu and Anael had ridden past over a month earlier, and then retreated to the west of the Rhine to fortify their position. When a week after their meeting with Gustaf they approached the Roman line, they were challenged by the soldiers there but ultimately allowed through when their general discovered that they were on business for the Guild. This was the first time that Nuadhu truly realised the influence that they had within the Empire, even though most people were unaware of their existence.

"We'll test that influence soon," Anael said when he remarked upon this. "Reaching a position whereby officials will turn a blind eye at the very mention of your name is one thing, but will the Empire answer to the Guild when they learn what's required to face the threat of the Adversary?"

"How could they not?"

"Easily enough, if there is no gain in it or it actively harms their interests."

"But it's in all our interests to defeat the Adversary's forces, they are the enemy of everyone."

"And if you haven't seen them first-hand, they are a concept that may or not be a real threat. It is easy enough to ignore a danger until it is at your doorstep, especially if you are involved in politics and statecraft."

Once they reached Augustodurum, Anael sought out Bricius to tell him what they had discovered. Nuadhu left her to that and went in search of his brother and Caoimhé.

He didn't have to look far. He found them inside the stable attached to the inn, where he was headed to tie up the horses, just as Pwyll put his lips to Caoimhé's. He was of a mind to leave them to it when one of the horses brayed loudly and stamped its feet, causing both to turn towards him with red faces.

They both stood where they were for several moments, staring, then at once they both ran towards Nuadhu calling his name. He greeted them each with an embrace, then beckoned them to follow him into the inn proper as he was saddle sore and needed to sit down.

"It appears that I wasn't the only one on an adventure then," he said, grinning when their blushes returned in force.

"Where have you been?" Caoimhé asked, in an attempt to deflect attention. "Where is Anael?"

"Anael has gone to tell Bricius what we discovered." Nuadhu answered. In response to their expectant stares, he detailed their journey east, what they had seen beyond the deserted villages, and how they had gotten back. He spent the most time detailing the enormous fort, with its different varieties of living dead inhabitants. By the time he was done, Pwyll and Caoimhé were engrossed and had forgotten their earlier embarrassment.

"So, what do we do now?" Pwyll asked.

"Fight back." Nuadhu told him. "Anael has always said that being Champion of Man means that I have to lead mankind against a great threat. Now we know what that threat is we have to defeat it."

"But why do you have to do that?" Caoimhé said. "The Roman Empire has the most powerful army in the world. Surely they can easily wipe out the Sons of Cain."

"Anael says that she doesn't know if they would, whether they would believe the threat or not in the first place to mobilise against it. But even if they did, they would only use that war as an excuse to expand their territory. The people of Germania don't want to be ruled by Rome any more than they want to be annihilated by the Sons of Cain. Or any more than we would want to be ruled."

"So, what do we do then?"

"We have to build an army of our own. Only an alliance of free men can defeat the power of the Adversary, where all who join us share a common interest in winning this fight and none have to look over their shoulder fearing subjugation in the event of victory."

"I see that the message has sunk in, then."

They all looked up from where they were sat to see Anael approaching.

"I've told Bricius what we saw," she said. "He shares my concerns over whether the Empire will act, but he insists that the Guild will press the matter robustly and raise it directly with emperor Tiberius if necessary. In the meantime, our concern as Nuadhu says is building an army to fight the Adversary, which Rome can join if it chooses to in time."

"How long do we have?" Pwyll asked. "Even with this kind of threat pressing down upon us, it will take a lot of time and effort to build an allegiance between the tribal chiefs."

"The Sons of Cain have been raiding villages over a considerable expanse, but they have been consolidating their territory slowly. Based on the reports that I have heard since we first arrived in Augustodurum and what we learned in Germania, I would guess that we have two years until the borders of the Empire are threatened.

"Perhaps longer, since they must know that once they make incursions here, they will not be dealing separate and often rival tribes but with territories which Rome is not going to let slip from its dominion lightly."

"Not to mention the barricades in Germania," Nuadhu

said. "They will surely hold for at least a while. The matter is urgent, but we do have time."

"In that time, you need to continue training me as a warrior. I need to be able to fight alongside my brother." As he had done often when he was younger, Pwyll puffed out his chest. The difference was that now, at the age of thirteen and on the verge of manhood, there was actually the threat of muscle when he did so.

Nuadhu smiled. "I would have it no other way, little brother."

"If Pwyll is to fight, then he will need me at his side." Caoimhé insisted, grabbing Pwyll's hand. Her face remained set and fierce, while Pwyll's flushed an even deeper red than before when Nuadhu had caught them kissing.

Anael looked at Nuadhu and raised an eyebrow, mirth in her eyes. "I've missed something, clearly."

Nuadhu shook his head, swallowing a laugh.

"Very well." She said, still smiling. "So, we're apparently agreed that everyone around this table is to be a warrior of great repute in this coming war. But we still need to address the matter of where you will begin building your army, Champion."

"That's easy enough." Nuadhu said, his face growing stern. "I will start by rallying my own people, the Brigantes. I have more chance of winning over the other chiefs if I am a chief myself."

Anael's own look was grave, fraught with worry. "And you intend to be one."

"I intend to take Judoc's place by challenging him to single combat. It is a sweet bonus that in doing so I will kill him and take my revenge for the death of my parents and the destruction of my village."

CHAPTER NINE

Bricius arranged for them to travel to Brigantia along with a Roman merchant who was taking slaves to trade at a market in Isuer. Although the disadvantage of this was that they would go north at a much slower pace, it meant that they were unlikely to be molested along the road, since Judoc was a fierce defender of trade relations with Rome.

Nuadhu was particularly unhappy with the arrangement. He accepted it as necessary due to the urgency of the situation, but his displeasure was plain on his face for much of the journey.

The merchant himself rode in an ornate wheelhouse, pulled along by his household slaves who rode on horseback. Several more were in the wheelhouse with him, waiting upon him as they trundled along. Outside of the vehicle, Anael, Nuadhu, Pwyll and Caoimhé as well as several free Romans flanked the party on horseback whilst the slaves going to market travelled on foot between them, watched over by a master with a whip and a sword, and burdened with packs of other goods being traded; spices, metals and so on.

Nuadhu's discomfort at their situation only grew, and more often he took to riding ahead or falling behind so that he didn't have to be near the caravan until they made camp at night. Though she could tell from his actions, Anael made a point of catching up with him after the first time he did it and asking what was wrong.

"Look at what we are riding with, Anael!" He said. "How can we hope to unite mankind together against the Adversary, to realise our common foe, when we still bind our fellow man in shackles? Would you suffer to live and die in the ownership of somebody else, forever at their mercy, worth no more than cattle or spices? Can you tell me that being taken as a slave by the forces of man is truly a better fate than being killed or granted immortality by the Sons of Cain?"

"Nuadhu…" She began, but then found that she didn't have the words to answer him.

"Tell the slaves of the world that they can have freedom, immortality and strength beyond measure, and they would flock to the Adversary's side!"

"But that is not the truth of it!" She insisted. "The Sons of Cain bear the shape of the men they were in life, but it is a different creature entirely inhabiting the body. The soul they displace spends eternity in Pandemonium, at the mercy of demons like that one which followed us through the forest when we first fled from Brigantia."

"Yes." For a moment, it seemed that she had stopped Nuadhu short, but then he recovered his flow. "But the fact that another fate is that much the worse doesn't mean this one is deserved. Am I the Champion of Man or just the Champion of those not in shackles?"

She agreed, entirely, with the argument he was making. In truth, she was proud of him for it since it was a conclusion he had come to of his own volition and against the popular consensus. But she couldn't say that. "The wrongs of slavery cannot be corrected if mankind is conquered. There will be others who fight for the soul of mankind, but for them to be able to do so you must first defend its body."

It was a weak argument and she knew it, but she drew her horse close enough to his to put a hand on his shoulder and look in his eyes. His own expression softened, and though he would ride off more times as they travelled north, for the moment he agreed to return to the caravan with her.

When they were in Brigantes territory and closing on Isuer, Nuadhu beckoned Anael, Pwyll and Caoimhé to ride off with him. When Anael objected that they should stay with the caravan to gain access to the hill fort, he insisted that it was only a short detour.

He led them to a lake in a relatively secluded area, surrounded on three sides by heavy forest. Once they had all dismounted, he led them down to the water.

"This area is one that warriors from our village would come to often." He said. "When they first took up sword and shield the druids of the faith would lead them here in prayer and then, as an offering to the gods of the forest, the warriors would dye and spike their hair. Caoimhé, you are the closest we have to a druid..."

"No. I was training to be a scholar and seer, not in faith or magic." She said, shaking her head.

"Don't worry, all I was going to ask is that you confirm me and Pwyll as warriors of Liuerpwl when we are done." Nuadhu said, offering her a kindly smile. "That is, presuming my brother still wishes to fight by my side?"

In an instant, Pwyll was stood next to Nuadhu, eager to begin.

"Anael." Nuadhu said.

"Yes?"

He blushed a little. "I've never done this before. Can you help?"

Anael nodded. She had, before the destruction of their town by Judoc, been witness more than once to warriors she helped to train having their hair bleached with lime and pulled up into spikes.

Nuadhu insisted that Pwyll have his hair dyed first,

much to the younger brother's delight. There were lime and clay deposits all around the lake, so it was easy enough to find enough to cover Pwyll's hair before washing it in the water. Once it came out white, she pulled it up into a tight braid on the back of his head.

Then it was Nuadhu's turn. She put a hand on his bare shoulder to hold him steady whilst she put the lime on his hair, but as she did, she felt goosebumps rise on his skin under her hand. She looked down at him and noticed pink in his cheeks. Then her eyes drifted down to his bare chest, broad and solidly muscled, with hair starting to grow across it, and felt her own face warm. She looked away, taking her hand of his shoulder and busying herself with bleaching his hair.

Once they were both done, Caoimhé presented each of them their swords in turn with the phrase, "Take this blade and stand now as a warrior of the Brigantes and of Liuerpwl." Then they donned their tunics and cloaks once more and rode back to the caravan.

As they went, she noticed Nuadhu casting furtive glances at her, but looking away hastily when she turned her head. This made her think back to the way that Pwyll had acted when Caoimhé had first joined them, but she tried to push it out of her mind. They had far bigger things to worry about than one awkward moment between them.

The layered earthen ramparts of Isuer came in sight a little over an hour after sunrise on their last day of travelling. They represented the grandest earthen works of the Briganti people, each tier standing fifty feet high and the wooden battlements at the top level surrounding the tribe's largest town and long hall. A moveable wooden bridge led across the ditch surrounding the fort, which was filled with sharpened stakes, and there were guards armed with spears and swords on either side.

The caravan stopped before the bridge and the merchant stepped out of the wheelhouse to present himself. His name was Pomponius, and he was a tall, balding man of considerable girth, though he had as much muscle on his chest and arms as he did fat on his stomach, making him appear almost oblong. He introduced himself and vouched for his company and his household slaves, the other slaves not needing accounting as they were goods to be sold at the market.

The guards barely spared them a glance before waving them on, the horses and then the wheelhouse following the path which wound around the fort up to the gateway on the top level. Once they were there, and again waved though by guards, the wheelhouse and horses were left with the stables before Pomponius and his company led the slaves to the market, leaving Anael, Nuadhu, Pwyll and Caoimhé to wander about freely.

"I will need to challenge Judoc publicly." Nuadhu said. "His actions in my town proved him a coward, so if he sees a way out, he will try to take it. But if the whole of Isuer sees the challenge, then a refusal would disgrace him."

"Yes," Anael agreed. "But still, be careful. When we fled him, it is almost certain that he was acting under the influence of demons, and we don't know how much that influence has grown in the past six years."

"No demon will save him." Nuadhu said simply.

They made their way into the centre of town, seeking out the market. Not only was this where most people were likely to be today, but Judoc and other high-ranking members of the tribe would almost certainly be among them. If Nuadhu's opportunity was going to come, it would be here, but the thought only made Anael feel tense.

When they arrived at the market, the numbers in attendance beyond the stall holders were sparse. Pomponius wasn't the only one lining up a row of slaves, though their conditions varied. Seeing one group of female slaves being made to stand naked, lash marks visible across their backs, made Anael feel physically sick. She instinctively looked to Nuadhu, who with gritted teeth and clenched fists urged them away from the slavers.

The market had brought in traders from across Britain as well as a number such as Pomponius from the Empire. Alongside slavers, there were horse traders, spice merchants, cloth merchants, smiths, food merchants and more.

The group split up and meandered about the stalls, talking to sellers and buyers as they waited for more people to arrive and for Judoc to make an appearance. Nuadhu kept his distance from the slavers, though his wariness of them was reflected in the rest of the group as well. Before mid-day, the market was thick with crowds and in amongst them were some of the highest-ranking tribespeople, wearing silver torcs around their necks.

Judoc appeared at noon, looking little different to how he had when Anael had last saw him six years before save for a thicker beard and more lines on his forehead. He rode into the market on horseback dragging two young men in shackles behind him. All trading stopped and everybody turned to watch as he dismounted and dragged them into the middle of the crowds. A space cleared around him.

"People of Isuer and Brigantia!" He bellowed. "Friends and visitors from across the world! You are fortunate today to bear witness to my rule and the law in action!"

He kicked each of the men in the back of the legs so that they fell to their knees. They were both Britons, most likely Brigantes, and of an important family based upon the patterns on their trousers. They were bare chested, with lashes across their chest and back.

"These men spoke treason and lies against me, for which I have deemed that they will die. Let this be a lesson to all – slander and plots against your king will not be suffered!"

"He is the liar!" One of them shouted.

Judoc's fist sent blood flying from his jaw.

"He consorts with demons!" The other yelled, before

he too was rewarded with a punch.

"So you see!" Judoc said, jabbing his finger in the men's direction. "Their own mouths betray their guilt! And you can rest assured, the guilty will always be punished!"

Nuadhu stepped forward. Anael had expected as much when she saw what was playing out, but her stomach lurched nonetheless. "Their only guilt is speaking the truth about you, Judoc!" He said.

Judoc's eyes were wild when he turned to the newcomer. "You are brave to speak out, turn-cloak!" He said. "Why do you think you can speak such treason in my presence and suffer no repercussions for it?"

Anael was aware of guards moving hastily around the crowd, but for now they kept their distance. Nuadhu advanced further into the open space cleared around Judoc and the condemned men. He now stood mere feet from the king of the Brigantes, one hand hovering next to his sheathed sword.

"I speak the words because they are truth. It is you who will suffer repercussions for your crimes."

The condemned men forgotten, Judoc stepped closer to Nuadhu with fists clenched. "Is that so? Who are you who presumes to judge your king?"

"You know me, Judoc. You gave me my name."

The whole crowd now watched in rapt silence. Both men spoke in low, harsh voices, yet you could hear every word.

"What name did I gave you, boy?" He jabbed Nuadhu in the chest. "Cease your nonsense and talk straight."

"My name is Nuadhu Iarraindorn, son of Caiside, warrior of Liuerpwl. I am here to seek vengeance for the parents you slaughtered and the town you razed."

Judoc visibly paled and took several steps back. It took him a moment to recompose himself. "No! You –" He barked laughter, short and sharp. "There is no vengeance for you here! Only death for your treason and the end of the threat that you pose to my people!"

"That is for the gods to decide." Nuadhu said. "If you think my vengeance undeserved, the lives of these men forfeit and your kingship just, then defend those claims with your sword. Judoc, son of Drustan and king of the Brigantes, I challenge you to single combat."

Judoc scowled at that. In the middle of the market, with so many watching, there was nothing he could do but accept the challenge.

CHAPTER TEN

They faced each other at dawn the next morning, in an open field beyond the hill fort. Judoc and Nuadhu stood ten feet apart from one another, each bare chested and with their skin decorated in blue woad. Both had their swords sheathed at their sides, waiting.

A significant crowd was gathered to watch the challenge, arranged in a semi-circle which gave the combatants a very wide berth. Anael was stood with Pwyll and Caoimhé, her stomach in knots. Her eyes were currently on the druid stood between Nuadhu and Judoc, a young man in a cowled robe bearing a golden staff. He was a law-speaker, whose responsibility it was not only to call the beginning of the contest but also to formally declare the victor and their prize.

"This man claims that I tried to kill him as a child and destroyed his village," Judoc called out as they waited. "In truth, he is an omen from the other-world. His presence here draws demons and evil spirits to us and places us all in danger. All true Brigantes, who love their tribe and wish their families to stay safe, have an interest in seeing him dead!"

"He lies!" Nuadhu called out in response. "There is a

darkness gathering in the east. It will come upon us either way, but I can lead us against it!"

The law-speaker druid raised his hands for silence. "We are all gathered here today to bear witness." He said. "Each of these men stakes a claim to justice and to the throne of Brigantia. They have agreed to pit their claims against one another in single combat. We call upon Belatucadros to guide their swords, and grant victory to the one who has the truest claim." With that he stepped back, and the fight was on.

Nuadhu drew his sword and adopted a fighting stance. Judoc drew and swung his sword in an arc over his head with a roar before advancing upon Nuadhu.

They got within two feet of each other before Nuadhu made the first strike. Judoc blocked quickly and the clash of their swords rang out in the air. They traded a rapid succession of blows. Nuadhu attacked while Judoc parried. Then Judoc went on the defensive. Nuadhu followed up with a further counterattack. Neither gave any ground, and they moved in circles as both refused to take any step back.

Judoc grinned and Nuadhu tensed. He bellowed as he made his next flurry of attacks. Judoc blocked them, but this time was clearly struggling, circling faster to avoid having to step back. The clash of iron against iron grew louder with each blow, Nuadhu continuing to holler and growl as he attacked.

Eventually, the king was forced to take several steps back. He blocked a last strike before side-stepping Nuadhu and withdrawing several paces.

"Impressive." The king said. "The woman taught you to fight, did she not?"

"Why, do you want some lessons?" Nuadhu shot back, with an edge to his voice.

Judoc shouted and attacked. Once more, the cry of the swords coming together rang out and for a short while the fury behind Judoc's attacks made it appear he had the upper hand.

But soon enough, Nuadhu recovered himself. He blocked and spun, sending Judoc staggering with an elbow to the side of his head. He managed to turn and parry just in time for Nuadhu's next strike, but then he was on the retreat as Nuadhu threw attack after attack at him, visibly struggling for breath and suffering the impact of each block.

By now, the crowd had warmed to Nuadhu, and there were shouts of 'Iarraindorn! Iarraindorn!' amongst the more general cheering and cursing as the fight went on. Anael's stomach was still lurching, joined by the hammering of her heart and what felt like the constriction of her rib cage, but it was now excitement as much as fear.

Nuadhu feinted low and then struck high, scoring a glancing blow to Judoc's temple. The king lurched and a hard slice at the hilt took the sword from his hand. Then Nuadhu kicked Judoc in the stomach, doubling him over, before shoving him to the floor.

Before he could strike a killing blow, Judoc scrambled backwards and leapt to his feet and ran to put distance between him and Nuadhu. Jeering followed him.

The shouting died when Judoc clenched his fist and fire erupted to surround it. He opened his hand in Nuadhu's direction, flinging the ball of flames at him. Nuadhu managed to spin out of the way, but the flames hit the ground just before the observers, sending a great number of them scattering and screaming.

Anael moved forward out of the crowd, but Nuadhu seemed to sense what she was going to do and turned towards her with a hand raised.

Another fireball came at him and he dodged it. Judoc roared with laughter.

"What's the matter, Iarraindorn? Have you lost your nerve?"

Nuadhu sheathed his sword and clenched his fists. Judoc laughed again. Nuadhu ran at him. Seven fireballs shot at him in quick succession, but he ducked or sidestepped as each one reached him, without losing his stride. Finally, he reached Judoc and threw his fist into the king's face. His jaw and nose exploded with blood a split second before he collapsed to the ground.

Judoc kicked out at Nuadhu, but he dodged it easily. As his opponent struggled to rise, he threw another punch, knocking him back down. Then he grabbed Judoc by the neck and hauled him to his feet. He threw punch after punch after punch to Judoc's head and chest, each crack or crunch loud to Anael's ears. Bruises appeared instantly and one cheek and half of his chest caved in on the impact of Nuadhu's fists.

Judoc was still standing, that very fact improbable, when Nuadhu drew his sword again and levelled it at the king's neck. "Any last words before you face the justice of the gods, Judoc?"

Judoc swayed on his feet, then met Nuadhu's eyes and forced a smile. "Yes." He said, his speech thick through broken teeth. "Ahriman, hear my prayer."

The crowd had now spread into a loose circle, everyone still watching the battle but no longer sure that they were just spectators. Their skittishness was rewarded with a blast of light and wind which knocked everybody down. Nuadhu flew several feet backwards through the air before crashing to the ground.

When the dust settled, Judoc still stood exactly where he had been. Only now he appeared taller and broader than he had been, all the wounds inflicted by Nuadhu gone and a pulsing, dark red glow about him.

He laughed and the voice was not his own, the sound a deep rumble which seemed to come from all around. "Did you really think it would be that easy, Iarraindorn?" He said. "I am the rightful king of the Brigantes, and I have the power of the gods behind me!"

"Ahriman is no god!" Nuadhu called back as he rose to his feet and unsheathed his sword. "What did you gain, in return for bartering your soul with the Adversary?"

Judoc spread his arms wide, grinning with what was now a mouth full of needle teeth. "What you see. The land, the power, the strength."

"So, the victory that brought you to the throne was your price? It seems a trifling fee for an eternity of torment and suffering in the darkest pits of the underworld."

"Enough chatter, Champion of Man. You came here to claim my life, but do you have the strength of body or will? Let us find out!"

With that, he stretched out his hand, and his sword came hurtling towards him from where he had dropped it on the ground. He caught the hilt, and flames roared up around the blade. He opened his other hand and a fireball appeared, hovering just above his skin.

"We have to help him!" Pwyll said.

Nuadhu heard him. "Stay back!" He called. "This is still single combat, and whatever tricks he pulls I can still beat him!"

In answer, Judoc hurled a fireball at him.

Nuadhu dodged it easily enough. But then Judoc swung his sword in a low arc, sending a long line of flames in his direction. He had to leap and twist to barely get out the way of it. As he pushed on forward, Judoc swung his sword this way and that, sending more and more lines of fire at Nuadhu from different angles, using his free hand to occasionally throw fireballs in between the lines.

At first, Nuadhu was able to keep moving forward. He leapt, ducked, spun and side-stepped to avoid the lines and balls of fire, though with considerable effort. But then Judoc got into his stride and it was all he could do to avoid getting burnt.

The audience was now well out of the line of fire, still watching but no longer cheering. They stared, silent and tense, as if unsure how they should react to this turn of events. In front of Anael, Pwyll and Caoimhé clutched each other's hands tightly, while all she could do was clench and unclench her fists, wishing that there were a way she could help Nuadhu.

Nuadhu was retreating now, sweat pouring off him and the woad on his body running in streaks. Judoc's attacks slowed and then stopped.

He spun his sword round in quick circles, the flames on the blade following in a spiral. Then he conjured another fireball with his free hand and shot it at the flames on the sword. Now, a wall of fire grew as it soared through the air towards Nuadhu. From where Anael stood, it looked too wide to dodge and too high to jump over.

But it was still moving in the air, its base not yet having touched the ground. Nuadhu ran at it and in that moment Anael thought that she would vomit. He dived, skidding on the grass and barely passing under the base of the wall before it touched the ground.

When it did, it singed the ground around it and continued to grow before exploding in a blast of heat that knocked a wide section of the crowd down, causing more than a few of them to pass out. One man caught fire and had to be shoved to the ground and covered in a cloak by those around him.

Despite all of this, Anael never took her eyes off Nuadhu. She was almost the only one who saw him roll under the wall of fire and fling his sword at Judoc. The blade spun so that only the flat caught him in the chest, but the sharp edge cut through a significant chunk of his forearm at the same time, a fountain of blood cascading out as the veins were split. The king stumbled and fell to his knees.

Nuadhu had no sooner launched the blade than he sprinted after it, and just as Judoc looked up after falling he sent him back to the ground with a hard right hook. Now he wasted no time and, in a moment, had his sword in hand. One clean swing separated Judoc's head from his shoulders.

The ground trembled and a black cloud rose from

Judoc's corpse, forming into the shadow of a creature with curved horns on its head and red glowing eyes. Anael pressed forward and drew her sword, recognising it for the Adversary. But it roared at Nuadhu before the cloud evaporated.

The next few moments passed in a stunned silence. Finally, the law-speaker druid recovered himself and approached Nuadhu.

"The result is clear, and Belatucadros has spoken through the swords of the combatants today." He said. "Judoc, son of Drustan, has been found guilty of consorting with demons and the destruction of Liuerpwl. His prisoners, his accusers, shall live.

"Now hail Nuadhu Iarraindorn, son of Caiside, Champion of Man and King of the Brigantes!"

Nuadhu raised his sword in the air. Cheers rose, and among them chants of "Hail! Hail!" and "Iarraindorn!"

Anael stood alongside Pwyll and Caoimhé, joining in the cheering and smiling. Her heart swelled with relief and pride. Nuadhu's muscles were taut, strained from his recent exertion and slick with sweat. As she watched him, drinking in his moment of vengeance and victory, she told herself that there was no desire mixed in among her other feelings.

ACT TWO:
MARCHING EAST

CHAPTER ELEVEN

After a year and a half of hard bargaining, Nuadhu stood at the southernmost shore of Britain with an army of twenty-five thousand behind him. There remained one more obstacle, however, before he could lead that army across the sea and eastward through Gaul.

The boat arriving now contained their best hope of making that passage peacefully, since after all this army hadn't been raised to fight other men. But the outcome of the discussion to come was still uncertain, and as his vessel reached the shoreline the face of the Roman proconsul gave nothing away.

He was dressed in his finest robes for the meeting, a relatively short man with a balding head and a thick neck. He was flanked by two centurions whose normal armour was topped by a yellow and red crest atop their helmets, and a standard bearer and ten legionaries followed in their wake. For the sake of diplomacy, Nuadhu had kept the bulk of his forces some distance away so as not to pose a direct threat, but still the proconsul cast his eyes across them with evident disdain.

Nuadhu himself looked every bit the king now. Having won his victory over Judoc, he had cut his hair short and wore it in tight spikes on his head. The silver and gold torc sat around his neck, while a dark cloak fastened with a golden brooch sat across his otherwise bare shoulders.

The other British tribes who had joined themselves to Nuadhu's cause were represented in command for the most part by the chiefs of their largest towns rather than by their kings. Though he had been able to adequately convince them of the danger, since word of Judoc's end had spread quickly, they were still wary of their own kingdoms being taken in their absence and so had elected to stay behind. The chiefs now stood in a line behind Nuadhu, while Anael, Pwyll and Caoimhé flanked him.

"Proconsul Quintus, thank you for coming." Nuadhu said in Latin, bowing his head.

Quintus bowed back at him. His escort kept a respectable distance, but from their formation it was clear that they were ready to move in should the proconsul be threatened.

"King Nuadhu." He said. "I suppose I needn't comment on how unusual this situation is, negotiating the incursion of your barbarian horde into my province."

A raised eyebrow was the only reaction that Nuadhu gave to the use of the phrase 'barbarian horde,' though Anael knew enough to recognise the tension in his jaw. It would be having to take the slight in good humour rather than the slight itself which grated upon him most.

"It is in everybody's interest that my 'horde' reaches Germania," he said, "And we have no wish for a war with Rome on the way."

"Well of course not," Quintus said with a smile that set Nuadhu's jaw again. "You can rest assured that all parties recognise that. The emperor himself has been appraised of the threat that we face, and he is convinced that Rome should not merely step aside for your crusade, but actively aid you in it."

"You will provide us with soldiers, then?"

"Yes. But that will be done once you reach Gaul.

Before then, I have been tasked with confirming the terms of your crossing."

"The terms should be simple enough. The men Rome provides, like all those the tribes have provided, remain under their original commanders. We make war against nobody except the Adversary and his army of living dead. When the war is done, we go home."

Quintus nodded. "Certainly, that covers most of it. However, there is also the matter of Brigantia." He gave the same smile as earlier. "You see, before you...replaced him, Judoc had established a particular relationship with Rome in regard to trade. Given the Empire's generosity concerning the current situation, we would of course expect that relationship to continue without interruption."

Nuadhu gritted his teeth. "Judoc's trade with Rome involved..."

"Slaves. Yes. I am aware of your actions since becoming king in this regard, which is of course your prerogative. But you must know that this cannot be replicated beyond your borders, and that it is not in your interest to try and stop the trade. Especially from Rome."

One of Nuadhu's first actions as king of the Brigantes had been to free all the slaves and insist that they be integrated into the tribe. This had initially caused unrest amongst the higher-ranking members of the tribe in particular, but Nuadhu had proven especially adept at convincing his people that they could not fight for the future of man while enslaving other men.

This had not gone down too well beyond the Brigantes, however, and Quintus was not the first person he had negotiated with to insist that he did not interfere with their right to take and trade slaves. He was the first, however, to insist that it be allowed in Nuadhu's territory.

Seeing Nuadhu tense, Anael took a hold of his shoulder and squeezed. Caoimhé stepped forward without having to be told and offered him her most disarming smile.

Sixteen now, Caoimhé had grown into an enchantingly beautiful woman. Her hair was a richer, darker red than it had been and her skin so pale that when she blushed it seemed like roses amid a snow drift, making her look like something more than human. She still wore the robes of a druid, having continued her training with the seers of the Brigantes, but it was the deep, green pools of her eyes, the fullness of her lips and the soft curve of her neck that drew the eye.

Quintus found his eyes drawn to the young woman, and when she touched his hand ever so lightly, he couldn't look away.

"Proconsul," she said, "My king will of course agree to explore the details of trade with Rome once this war is done. But we are surely not best placed to agree to more than that while we are about to take an army across the water."

Quintus blinked several times. "No." He said. "No, of course not. The commitment to discuss the matter in more depth will of course suffice. In the meantime, I shall make sure that our men are ready to join you in Gaul."

There were some more formalities to be observed, including introducing the proconsul to the chiefs and allowing him to view the gathered army. However, with Caoimhé's intervention the agreement for them to travel across to Gaul was settled and then Quintus and his escort had returned to their boat and were making their way home.

"That was some trick," Nuadhu said to Caoimhé once Quintus had gone. "I didn't realise that you were able to do mental manipulation like that."

Caoimhé smiled. "I'm not. But some of us do have skill in diplomacy, even if you don't."

"Diplomacy?"

"He would never refuse you passage through Gaul. As he said, Rome is well aware of the danger that we all face, as well as the fact that you are the best placed to defeat that threat. All Quintus could do was make you feel like you were backed into a corner, and without my diplomacy you would have been – angry but knowing that you couldn't risk being unable to cross the water."

She shrugged, then turned away from Nuadhu and grabbed Pwyll, pulling him into a kiss.

"It's easy to see why Pwyll likes her," Anael said to Nuadhu.

Nuadhu shrugged. "Most women in Britain have a similar level of sexual confidence."

"That's not what I – how would you know?"

Nuadhu flinched, and Anael blushed when she realised how she had reacted.

"Sorry."

"You meant her quick thinking and intellect." He smiled. "It was meant as a joke."

"Sorry." She repeated.

He put an arm around her shoulders and gave her a squeeze. Again, she blushed. In the last year and a half, the negotiations to unite the tribes had occupied enough of their time that she hadn't had to think about her feelings for him. But now as he embraced her, the skin along her shoulders and arms raised in goosebumps, all the conflicting thoughts she had been holding back filled her head.

She shrugged his arm off. "Come on," she said to change the subject, "We need to get our army across the sea to Gaul."

It would take them four days to get the entire army onto boats and across the sea from Britain to Gaul. They arrived several miles to the north east of Augustodurum and made their camp there while Nuadhu and Anael rode to the town to meet with Bricius.

He met them by the amphitheatre. Although he hadn't seen her in more than a year, he greeted Anael in the usual over-familiar way of his adopted persona. She could almost feel how tense Nuadhu became on seeing this.

Bricius seemed to sense it too, and he withdrew hastily before beckoning them to follow him into the amphitheatre and down to the underground room where he had taken Anael on their first meeting.

"What news do you have for us?" Anael asked once they were there.

"The Sons of Cain have not breached the border that the Germanic tribes built." Bricius said. "But we have no reason to believe that they are in any way hampered by it. Rather, our sources say that they are advancing east into Sarmatia."

"Why?" Nuadhu asked.

"Rome has conquered a quarter of the known world, but that still leaves three quarters of the world beyond its reach. The people there are targets of the Sons of Cain as much as the rest of us, and the more of them are turned when they advance upon the empire the harder they will be to defeat."

"It won't come to that. We will take the battle to them and tear apart the territory they've built."

"Yes, and just as Rome will be providing soldiers to help you do that, the Guild wishes to do our part too."

"I thought the Guild was part of the Empire?"

"We operate within it and we have the ear of the emperor, but we are and always have been a separate entity. We have our own organisation and we are more than prepared to match our strength to yours. But we can offer you more than just soldiers."

There was a click and the hidden door at the end of the room swung open. From it, emerged five men and two women. They were all dressed in Roman-style plate armour and red cloaks.

"It was the original founders of the Guild who created the first Champion of Man, as I'm sure Anael has told you." Bricius said. "But what she may not have told you, or may not know, is that that was not the last time that the Guild's warlocks used their magic to make great warriors into something more. But, unlike the Champion who appears only in times of great crisis, they tied this magic to bloodlines so that the descendants of those first warriors would carry on their duties."

He gestured to the seven stood at the back of the room. "Nuadhu, Anael, may I introduce you to Gaius Cantius Balbus, Aelia Helvetia Musa, Titus Salvius Lurio, Sabina Vinicia Arvina, Decimus Quirinius Momus, Marcus Lucretius Rectus, and Agrippa Hirtius Avitus. They are the current descendants of those original warriors, the seven Sentinels."

Each of the warriors bowed their heads in turn when introduced.

Anael surveyed them, each standing at rigid attention for inspection, then turned back to Bricius. "So these...Sentinels...each have the strength of a Champion of Man?"

"I suspect not quite, as the magics used to create the Sentinels were different to that used to create the Champion. I am told that the original spell was quite unique and cannot be recreated. But still, they have a strength beyond the human, and they are well trained and battle tested. They will be the captains of the units we provide to you, and I would advise that you make full use of them in this campaign."

"Very well," Anael said, "but why was I not aware of them before now?"

"Because there are always other threats to be dealt with, even while you await a world ending crisis. Most recently, they had been destroying a particularly large lycanthrope pack in the African province."

"I see." But Anael was thinking back to her time with previous Champions, and instances when the support of these Sentinels would have been invaluable. She pushed the thoughts aside, though they lingered at the back of her mind. "We thank the Guild for its support, as we will need every advantage we can get if we are to have a hope of defeating the Adversary."

It was a further week before, with the additional numbers provided by Rome and the Guild, the army that would make a stand for humanity formed up ready to march. Sixty thousand in total, the majority infantry but with a substantial cavalry from the Roman detachment and a fair number of chariots at the edge of the British ranks. The Guild's forces formed up alongside the Romans, in similar armour and distinguished only by the white pentacle on black held up by their standard bearers.

On horseback at the front of this great mass, Nuadhu looked back and surveyed the forces that he would be leading to the east into the realm of the Sons of Cain.

"It's a formidable force," Pwyll said. "And they could ask for no better commander."

Nuadhu smiled. "Let us hope so, brother. We ride against all the might of the underworld, and if we fail then mankind is forfeit."

With that, he signalled and the army began its march east.

CHAPTER TWELVE

By the time that the army was fully on the move, it formed a vast, slow moving column. Those on horseback and in chariot were hampered by the speed of the infantry, who in turn were held back by the wheelhouses. On the Roman roads, they made twenty miles a day, but once they passed the borders of the empire, their progress slowed by half.

It took two months to enter Germania and reach the barricades built to stop the advance of the Sons of Cain. On their way, they found the villages that they passed empty. However, it soon became clear why when on the last leg of their journey to the barricades they ran into a force of ten thousand Germanic warriors.

Nuadhu called a halt and rode out to parley with their leader. It turned out to be Gustaf, who called out cheerfully when he recognised that his opposite was Nuadhu.

"Nuadhu! Hail!" He said. "I was beginning to think you would never return."

"I told you that I had duties to attend to, Gustaf."

Gustaf looked at the army beyond him. "Ah, and this was your duty, yes? I trust that you are here to make war upon the Adversary rather than to conquer my people!"

He laughed.

Nuadhu smiled. "Of course, my friend! And I would be most grateful if you chose to marry your strength to ours. We must march east to face the Adversary and tear down his empire, and the more of us stand together the better chance we have."

"Then it appears that we must march with you!" Gustaf agreed.

There was a delay of several more days as Gustaf sought the agreement of all the other clan chieftains, and they made a passage across the barricade onto the other side. The Germanic tribes added fifteen thousand to the numbers under Nuadhu's command, while leaving a further five thousand behind at the barricade to ensure it was well defended.

Once they were moving again, the army's progress was even slower than it had been before. Though now they were in the territory abandoned to the Adversary, there were still many uneventful days of marching through woodlands and passing abandoned villages.

It was the middle of the morning when outriders finally came back to report that they were within a day's march of the fort that Nuadhu and Anael had come across almost two years earlier. When the news came, Nuadhu immediately called a halt to the march and convened a meeting of the war council. It took place in the open air as the camp was still being set up.

The council comprised his brother, Caoimhé, Anael, the Sentinels, the British and Germanic chiefs, and the Roman commanders. They numbered almost forty when assembled and tended to talk over one another which often led to arguments, so Nuadhu had learned quickly when to cut in and when to bring the councils to an end. But this was the first time that the need to make a strategic decision had presented itself.

No sooner had he finished laying out his plan than there was an uproar. He let it go on for close to a minute, surveying the room and making note of who was objecting the loudest before he said "Enough" in a voice loud enough to bring everybody back to silence.

"I realise that the plan presents its share of dangers," he said, "but this is only the first obstacle of this campaign and we do not know how far the Sons of Cain's territory expands to the east. They will almost certainly know that we are marching upon them soon enough, if they don't already, but in the meantime we should use the element of surprise while we can."

"Yes," a British chief called out, "but this is not surprise, it is madness!"

A rush of others clamoured to agree.

"The plan has potential," Gustaf put in, "and if it fails, we will still be able to fall back to siege machinery."

"Those undertaking the mission will have to be warriors of unequalled skill," a Roman commander countered, "but if there is a high chance that this will not work, that is a resource we can ill afford to lose!"

Nuadhu let the debate go on, the supporters and opponents of his plan now easier to discern than before. He was determined to go through with it, and he was aware that some of those opposed simply didn't want to try it. But he noted carefully the very real pitfalls that the plan could face, so that he could anticipate them.

"I like this plan." Said Musa, a female sentinel with dark brown skin, close cropped hair and arms rippling with muscles. A white scar bisected her cheek from just below her left eye. "But as has been pointed out it will require exceptional skill to carry out. I will lead this mission."

Nuadhu smiled. "Now we're getting somewhere. I will be leading this mission, but you can be part of it. I need two more volunteers."

More uproar. At his side, Anael touched his shoulder and gestured to indicate that she would volunteer. He shook his head. "I need you here, ready to give the command when I signal that we have succeeded."

She held his gaze, the expression on her face familiar enough to him that he knew she didn't like the idea and was already worrying for him. He took her hand in his and squeezed before saying "I will succeed." She smiled in return, though again he knew that she was only pretending to be reassured. His stomach fluttered and he pulled his hand away, turning back to the council to distract himself.

After the shouting died down again, he accepted two more volunteers in Gustaf and a young British chief called Cynbel.

"The matter is settled then." He told the council. "The four of us will go on ahead once the sun sets this evening, and on Anael's command our army will follow when we have succeeded."

Anael waited until the council was dispersed and they were alone before grabbing him by the shoulders to stop him from walking away.

"This plan is very dangerous." She said.

"We are at war, Anael. There are risks everywhere."

"That's not what I meant, and you know it."

He sighed and took both of her hands. He could feel them trembling. "It is dangerous, but it is not at all impossible. I will succeed in this and we will march on triumphant, I promise you."

"You had better." She smiled now, more genuine than earlier in the council.

"I will always come back to you, Anael."

She leaned in to kiss him and his heart stopped. Before their lips met, however, a bird screeched overhead. They both jumped and looked up. The crow cawed again, stopping directly overhead and flapping its wings frantically before setting off again.

Nuadhu's heart was hammering in his chest. He looked back at Anael, she smiled, and then they both burst out laughing.

"Come back." She reminded him, before walking away.

When dusk came, Nuadhu, Musa, Gustaf and Cynbel

saddled up their horses and set off. Unlike on his original journey with Anael, Nuadhu avoided the thickest part of the forest and led them along a game trail going in the rough direction of the fort. By the time they reached it, it was full dark and the sky was thick with clouds, making it difficult to see too far ahead. The wind howled, blowing away from the castle towards them, and with it a bite of cold they wouldn't have otherwise felt.

They tied up the horses out of sight of the battlements, before moving forward on foot. Once their eyes adjusted to the darkness, they were afforded a black and white view of their surroundings. There appeared to be nobody around, however, and the flaming torches lit on the battlements would make it harder rather than easier for sentries to see their approach. Still, they waited until the nearest sentry was looking the other way before crossing open ground to press themselves against the wall.

Nuadhu passed Musa a length of rope and she gave him a grin that stretched out her scar. Then she slung the rope over her shoulder and started climbing. Every movement was deliberate and carefully weighed, yet also quick. She found handholds and footholds quicker than Nuadhu could have scanned the stones ahead of him and soon enough she was high up and hard to see against the wall in the darkness.

Several minutes passed in silence. Then there was the scraping of iron on stone that could only be the portcullis opening. Nuadhu beckoned everyone quickly around the side of the fort, and they got out of sight just before a small troop of riders went past. There must have been thirty in total, heading west.

"They will see our horses!" Gustaf said.

"There's nothing we can do about that." Nuadhu told him. "We have to carry on."

They returned to the spot where they had been before the portcullis opened. A minute or so after that, there was a heavy thud somewhere up above, and they looked up to see the rope being lowered – with one end knotted in the thick hair of a severed head. Its owner had been a Son of Cain, its face now permanently fixed in a red-eyed, sunken-cheeked glower.

They waited for the head to reach the ground, then Cynbel climbed up followed by Gustaf. Finally, Nuadhu followed them. At the top, he found the other end of the rope tied to the headless body. Another decapitated corpse, this one with its head lying in close vicinity, could just be made out further along the battlements. Musa was stood close by, her blade still dripping with blood. When they were all up, she beckoned, and they kept low to follow her along the battlements. Within them, the main keep now stood complete, Nuadhu noted, with the scaffold gone.

Once they found stairs leading down to the ground, Gustaf peered over and was able to spot three sentries at different points within the outer wall. He signalled for the others to wait and then, after watching for close to a minute, he descended the stairs slowly, crouched low, with his weapon drawn.

It was close on five minutes later when they heard a cry, quickly silenced, and then eventually Gustaf reappeared to lead them down.

"The last one of them caught my scent when I got close, like a wolf or a hound." He said. "With the others, I think we were lucky due to the direction of the wind. We will have to tread carefully and be prepared to make our stand once discovered."

Once they were inside the keep, however, they found it almost entirely empty. A quick search of the ground floor found what appeared to be a great hall, with a throne on a dais at the far end, but there was nobody around it. With nothing else to be seen, they made their way down to the dungeons.

As soon as they stepped down the stairs, the smell hit them. Excrement and sweat were particularly in strong in the noxious mix of odours that filled the air and made the eyes water. The corridor they came into was almost black, lit only by one torch in a sconce at either end, with the cells in between, and as they reached them the smell became so overwhelming that Nuadhu thought he might gag.

It soon became apparent why. In the cell to the right, the mass of people crowded together looked starved and barely human. Nuadhu brought a torch closer to them and they shied away from it, their skin grey and stretched tight over bones with no flesh to hide their outline. Their eyes were pinholes, long accustomed to near darkness. They were covered in a layer of dirt, their clothes reduced to shapeless rags, and the line of buckets at the back of the cell overflowing with dark liquid.

There was a corpse lying next to them, putrefying with maggots crawling out of its eyes and mouth. One of them, who might have been a woman once, cradled a baby which couldn't possibly be still alive from the angle of its head. Nuadhu turned his head away sharply.

"Death would be a mercy for those wretched souls," Cynbel said.

Nuadhu didn't reply, only moved over to the opposite cell. This one was cleaner, and its occupants looked much fresher and new to the darkness. There were nine of them, all men but for one woman and all strong looking adults. Their wounds were fresh and there was hope in their eyes when they saw the torch.

Next to them, however, lay a row of corpses. These, too, were fresh and the only wound was the bite at their necks.

"Prisoners! How long have you been here?" Nuadhu asked in a hushed voice.

"A day, perhaps two." A man answered. "Our village lies to the north and we had repelled them several times before, but this time we failed."

"And the dead men – did you see them die?"

"Yes. The, those creatures bit their throats and drank their blood."

"Did they offer the victims their own blood?"

"What? I don't... yes. They cut open their wrists and made them drink before leaving them for dead. They seemed weak afterwards."

"We're going to get you out of there. But keep well clear of the bodies, lest they rise."

The prisoners stood up and backed off as Nuadhu examined the door.

Then the sound of footsteps and muted voices carried down the stairs. Everybody tensed. The other prisoners, behind him, started wailing in low, weak voices. Nuadhu ordered Musa, Cynbel and Gustaf to cover him. He grasped the lock.

"Shut up!" Someone shouted, still out of sight on the stairs. "That noise, it grates upon me."

"These creatures are one step from ghouls." Another voice answered. "Why we keep them alive..."

Then they came into view, two Germanic warriors with armour covering their furs. When they saw the three warriors facing them, their hands went to their swords, while their faces changed to reveal them as Sons of Cain. Musa led the advance upon them, with Cynbel and Gustaf close behind her.

Nuadhu didn't have time to watch the battle, as in front of him the first of the dead started to stir. He raised his sword and brought it down as hard as he physically could, shattering the lock and sending the door swinging open.

The first corpse had sat up now. He took its head as it turned to face him, then decapitated the other dead still lying on the ground. After a moment of hesitation, the prisoners followed him out of the cell. He glanced over at the other cell and saw the prisoners within staring at him as blankly as before, unmoving. He used his blade to break their lock, but none of them reacted in the slightest to the door opening.

He knew that they were beyond help, and the sight of them made his stomach turn, so he moved on. Once they had taken the fort, they could decide what to do with these poor, wretched creatures.

By the time Nuadhu reached the skirmish further ahead, the enemy was already dead. He shared a look with Musa.

"I've never seen a fort like this before. It shouldn't be this easy to capture."

Cynbel slapped him on the shoulder. "Worry not, Iarraindorn! There will without doubt be more enemies for you to vanquish in time!"

Yet there were no more to be found in the dungeon, on the ground floor or in the higher levels of the keep. The only other inhabitants they encountered were a few walking corpses tending to the large, empty bedrooms that sat upstairs. They cowered in terror at the sight of armed intruders, a peculiar sight that made Nuadhu feel slightly bad when they put the revenants out of their misery.

Then all that was left to do was to inform the rest of the army that the fort was taken. There were several horses tied up in stables outside the keep, and Gustaf took the healthy freed prisoners back with him to the camp.

It was four hours before he returned, with the camp having to be broken down before they could move on. When they arrived, they made camp outside of the stone ramparts as though settling in for a siege and Nuadhu came out to meet them. He presented Musa as the victor of the day, and cheers rang out from the army, who were still yet to see real combat.

"I think those enemy riders expected to find a small raiding party." Anael told Nuadhu, after they embraced. "We took them by surprise and have kept two of them alive for interrogation. But so far all he will tell us that their numbers approach a million and he claims that Cain himself leads them."

"Cain. The father of these creatures?"

"The Adversary is their true father, but yes, Cain was the first and the one from whom all others can claim descent. But I saw him die myself, centuries ago, so he cannot be their leader."

"Their leader is beside the point if they now number close to a million."

"Yes, but I have my doubts about that claim, too."

"We will know the truth soon enough. I intend to leave a small garrison here, so that if we are forced to fall back then we have a point to hold. But ultimately, we need to keep pressing on and destroy their entire empire, and every last one of the Sons of Cain with it."

"A bold ambition."

"A necessary one, or the alternative is our annihilation."

Looking at Anael then, he wanted to reach out and caress her. But the moment that had presented itself the day before had long passed. He excused himself to find out if his tent was being set up.

Before dawn the next morning, the camp awoke to the blaring of horns in the distance. *A-hooooooooooo. A-hooooooooooo.* Nuadhu ordered that they break camp and form up straight away. Several minutes after that, the outriders who had camped a mile or so ahead of the main column came riding back at a furious gallop.

"What news?" Nuadhu asked them.

"The enemy, my king." One of the scouts answered. "Perhaps twenty thousand, marching our way."

"We greatly outnumber them," Pwyll said, having just appeared at his brother's side. "This will be an easy victory."

"Not one among them is human," Nuadhu reminded him. "There will be nothing easy about this. Whatever losses we suffer, we cannot recoup, and this will not be the sum of the Adversary's forces by a long way."

Nonetheless, he summoned his commanders and started giving out orders. However much he disliked the situation, battle was upon them and they had no choice but to fight.

CHAPTER THIRTEEN

The sound of the horns continued to ring in the air, yet it would be over two hours before the opposing army finally came in sight. In that time, the commanders charged off to bellow orders at their forces, following Nuadhu's direction as hastily as they could. Nuadhu himself advanced the front line forward to dictate where they would meet the enemy.

The cliff-side upon which the fort was built carried on beyond the structure in a wide arc which left few paths north and none that could be traversed by an army. The forest facing it was so dense that it was almost impassable itself, and certainly wasn't something you could lead a large body of men through. However, beyond the fort a wide clearing opened between these two natural barriers.

"We should use the fort," Anael insisted. "Otherwise we're just thrusting warriors into the jaws of death and hoping that the sheer volume will choke them."

"We can't fit everyone inside and the terrain in the shadow of the fort is unfit for a battle. Not to mention that they know the fort better than us and we haven't had the time to check for hidden passages and ways in." He turned to her and smiled. "I know what I'm doing. Have faith."

She did have faith, she wanted to tell him, but that wouldn't stop her from worrying. Instead, she took his hand and squeezed it tight before riding off to take her own position.

The British chariots were at the front of the formation, each carrying two warriors besides the rider. One of them was an archer with an oil-soaked wrapping around their arrowheads, and the other a swordsman who also carried a hot brand. Behind them, the cavalry, and behind them the infantry. There were thirty thousand in total, half of the army absent and the archers beyond those on the chariots nowhere to be seen.

When the enemy came into sight, it was immediately clear that they were not simply playing a numbers game. The opposing side had a cavalry, but it was extremely small and most of the army was on foot. However, running in amongst them were enormous black dogs that stood four feet high when on all fours, with horns on their heads and fire in their eyes. The sound of their growling was far removed from the barking of ordinary dogs, ferocious and terrible.

Her horse whickered nervously as it caught the creatures' scents. It wasn't the only one. Anael tried to calm her steed and shot a look at Nuadhu. He caught her gaze and smiled.

This didn't exactly put her at ease, especially as the enemy now broke into a charge and the cavalry halved the distance between the two sides without Nuadhu reacting. Finally, however, he raised his sword.

"Archers! Draw!"

The command was repeated up and down the line.

"Ignite!"

Brands were set to arrowheads so that they caught fire.

"Loose!"

Flaming arrows soared from the human front line in the direction of the Sons of Cain. This made their horses rear and halted their advance, screams, shouting and yelps reaching her ears as the arrows hit.

Immediately, the archers drew a fresh set of arrows. But even as they did, more arrows rained down upon the enemy, this time from the forest. Anael glanced back at Nuadhu, whose grin was even wider since he had obviously anticipated this, and sent the archers ahead to find positions within the trees. She rolled her eyes and turned her attention back to the fray.

Several more rounds of arrows fell upon the enemy, leaving the battlefield charred and smoking. As the chariot archers' shots landed, the forest archers would fire, and vice versa.

But while this hail took out many of the enemy horses and horned dogs, even those Sons of Cain who were impaled or set on fire survived, since only taking their head off their shoulders could end their lives. Soon enough, they would regroup and simply charge on through the flames towards their human enemy.

Nuadhu ordered the chariots forward. Arrows continued to fire from the back of the carts, as they rode towards and along the enemy lines. The swordsmen thrust and stabbed at any opponent who came too close, while the horses dragged them in wide, looping paths that were difficult to predict.

Anael saw enemies leaping through the flames and jumping on several of the chariot horses. One slashed at the animal while another attacked the rider. But she didn't see what followed as Nuadhu ordered the cavalry in and a moment later she was galloping forward with her sword drawn. She reached the heat of the battle within moments, and the panorama she had had of the whole battle vanished so that all she could see was where she needed to dodge or strike next.

Her horse continued to snort and whine as it ran, aware that it was in a potentially fatal situation. Here, she pulled it up short of a black dog and leaned to slash at the creature when it pounced. There, one of the Sons of Cain leapt at her from the side and the parry would have knocked her from the saddle had the horse not come to a halt. She never saw where the attacker went.

Ahead, another enemy still on horseback charged at her. They sparred and parried, turning and charging at each other several times before she caught him in the throat and dragged him off his steed. The animal did the rest, stamping on his neck as it reared and tried to flee.

She caught only glimpses of the rest of the battle around her. A clean decapitation with a sword. Needle teeth tearing at flesh. Several black dogs dragging a screaming horse to the ground. Hoofs trampling over bloody fur. There were fires here and there, and much of the grass was smoking. Screaming, shouting, roars and grows filled her ears.

The infantry was in the thick of the battle now. She hadn't heard the order, wasn't even sure when it had been given. All that she was aware of was the dance of her horse as she steered it through hazards all around and the weight of her sword as she swung and thrust.

The sky brightened as the morning wore on, but there was no other indicator of time passing or progress in the battle. Foes kept coming from all directions, leaping and snarling as they did, with no suggestion that they were thinning in number. When she caught glimpses of others from her own side there was no way to tell if they were falling faster than the enemy or vice versa. Yet still bodies littered the ground.

At least one that she moved over wasn't dead, and the sound her horse made as its belly was ripped open was terrible. She leapt off and thrust her sword, catching what turned out to be a black dog in the jaw. After she finished it off, she cut her horse's throat as a mercy to end the animal's suffering.

On foot, the throng was thicker and the battle more intense. The horse had given her an amount of space that no longer existed, so that all she could do was cleave and hack to keep the swords and the teeth at bay. Learning from the horse's mistake, she stepped around rather than over corpses. The foe she was fighting was never in the centre of her vision, as she was always watching her footing and her surroundings for more enemies.

Two Sons of Cain were hacking at her from opposite sides when the ground shook. She lost her footing and stumbled just as she was turning from one to the other. The one behind her swung its sword, but the shaking only intensified and it missed by a wide margin. Anael drove her sword through the chin of the one in front of her, then hacked at the chest of the one behind. She kicked, shoved and sliced her way out into open space to see what was going on.

The fort on the mountainside was visibly trembling against the sky with the shaking of the ground. Smoke seeped from the edges where the walls met the rock. Moments later, the small garrison Nuadhu had left inside came running out of the front.

The remains of the camp were still visible where they came out, but there was nobody to be seen there. Casting about quickly, Anael didn't think that any more of their numbers had joined the fray than had been initially formed up before the Sons of Cain charged. But of the rest of their army there was no sign.

The shaking continued to intensify, causing everybody to lose their footing and effectively calling a halt to the fighting as everybody struggled to right themselves. The smoke coming from the mountain was thick, black, and the air was growing thick with soot.

There was a rolling crash, like a clap of thunder and heavy waves hitting a cliff wall at the same time. The fort didn't collapse or explode so much as vanish, dropping from sight as a cloud of dust enveloped it. Immediately, the shaking stopped and as though a veil had been lifted the fighting and shouting resumed as quickly as it had ceased.

Anael parried an attack to her right and then another behind her, but she didn't head back into the fray. Instead she forced her way out of it in the direction of the mountain. A sense of urgency pulled at her about the collapse.

A black dog leapt on her back and forced her to the ground. Its breath was hot on the back of her neck. She kicked and thrashed, but its weight was too much and she couldn't shift it. Then it fell limp and collapsed on top of her. A moment later it was gone. She looked up and saw Caoimhé offering her hand.

"Thanks." Anael said as she stood up.

"Be more careful next time." Caoimhé said, before raising her sword and re-entering the fight.

The dust had cleared to reveal a smoking hole in the mountainside where the castle had been. Already, she could see a mass of thousands coming out from it, and they could only be reinforcements for the Sons of Cain army. The first ones to climb through the rubble onto firmer ground bellowed and broke into a run.

Anael glanced around. The battle was moving away from her, several feet now lying between her and the nearest combatants. Able to see the whole field at once now, as opposed to the snapshots she had been granted within the fray, it was clear that the humans continued to outnumber the Sons of Cain and, despite the agility and strength of the enemy, were overwhelming them.

But they were facing the wrong way, and with the numbers pouring out of the cave it would be the humans who were outnumbered and overwhelmed. Where was the rest of their army?

Her question was answered when an enormous, flaming projectile flew at the rubble of the castle, crushing a great number of the enemy. Several moments later, another followed it while the flames of the first were still crackling. The sound of the impacts and the screaming that followed stopped the charge of the reinforcements, as many of them looked back and then stopped when they saw what was happening.

A third projectile crashed directly into the rubble at the mouth of the cave, sending rocks flying in all directions as well as setting the enemy afire. Only then did the catapult come into view, an extremely hasty construction, the main throwing arm attached to a rope which required a line of warriors to pull down hard to operate. The rope was slack now as another projectile of rock, rubble and wood was loaded.

Those already out of the cave were too slow to react. The catapult turned to them, and in a necessarily well-timed move the projectile was doused in oil and set alight less than a second before the men pulled the rope on the throwing arm down. It caught fire in mid-air before landing amidst them and shattering apart into flaming pieces which shot in all directions.

A collective bellowing signalled the arrival of the rest of the human army, who came storming out of the forest to the west with swords and axes raised. Those surrounding the catapult abandoned it to draw their weapons and join the charge.

Finally, the reinforcements regained their senses and ran to meet the ambush head on, including a number who had survived in the tunnel coming out to join their comrades.

Anael didn't wait to see the two sides meet, but turned and forced herself back into the original battle. The sooner that they defeated the first tranche of the enemy, then they could all join themselves to the new fight and finish it off together.

A black dog leapt at her. She ducked and skewered it in the gut. She dragged her sword from its carcass into the face of a Son of Cain. It thrashed and screeched. She took its head. Another tried to cut her in two with a pair of battle axes. She barely dodged. A succession of violent swings came. She blocked, ducked and sidestepped. The enemy turned too slow. His neck sliced clean.

She fought now with a renewed vigour. Her sword felt light, the momentum carrying her through from one attack to the next. From one enemy to another. Sons of Cain and black dogs alike fell under her attacks. Now she could see their numbers thinning. The human numbers appearing to grow as the enemy fell all around.

The sun was at its height, signalling that it was midday, when finally there were no more enemies to fight. A silence fell as everybody looked around them, taking in the carnage and the piles of bodies on the floor, drinking in the fact that they had survived.

Then a cheer broke. It came from the west, in the shadow of the fort reduced to rubble. There, thirty thousand humans stood over the broken corpses of their enemies. The roar of their victory was infectious, and it soon spread amongst the other mass of humans who a few hours earlier might have been on the verge of losing.

Anael's body was soaked through with sweat. She wanted nothing more to collapse and relieve the burden of her feet, but she couldn't do that until there wasn't a sea of corpses around her. So instead she moved through the crowd, searching.

She found Pwyll first, blood spattered across his bare chest and his sword hanging limply in his arm. He looked at her and smiled, but she got the sense that he might not have been seeing more than the sun in the sky, given how exhausted he looked. She took him by the arm and brought him with her.

When they found Caoimhé, she and Pwyll embraced and kissed almost frantically. Anael gave them their moment, then clapped Caoimhé on the shoulder and thanked her for saving her life.

After many more minutes of looking, made harder by the fact that others were also moving about trying to find those that they knew and had come to war with, there was still no sign of Nuadhu. Anael didn't want to look down, as she feared seeing his face on the ground. But a knot was growing in her stomach as she wondered if something terrible had happened to him after all.

Then she heard the shout, some distance away and faint. She couldn't quite tell, but she thought it might have been his voice and her name. She was wrong, and her heart sunk as she saw it was instead one brother calling out the name of another in grief. The face of the dead man was almost identical to that of the man who was on his knees clutching the body and crying.

Then a hand touched her shoulder and she jumped. She turned and saw it was Nuadhu. He smiled at her, and she cried out, pulled him close and kissed him on the lips. When she pulled away and saw the reaction of shock and confusion on his face, she laughed and felt her cheeks warming.

"I'm sorry." She said. "I couldn't find you. I thought you were…"

"I'm fine." He promised, with a hand on her arm. "I told you to have faith."

She looked over at the rubble that had been the fort. "How did you know?"

"I didn't. I guessed that the Adversary would be aware of our presence and would try to get rid of us as quickly as he could. But I never thought…I'm still not sure how his army could have burrowed through the mountain or destroyed the fort so effectively."

"Magic, I'm sure. We're just lucky that you were anticipating something."

"Yes. But this has also highlighted that we cannot simply march onward in a conventional campaign. We must think differently, and this will take a lot longer than originally anticipated."

"What do you mean?"

"I have been thinking of this in far too conventional terms. This will not simply be a case of our army marching against the Adversary's and then taking his capital. No doubt his army will have to be vanquished to stop him advancing further, but he has been very deliberate in every step he has taken to seize this land from man, and in reclaiming it we must be the same.

"There must be no chance that the Sons of Cain can reform into a new army, with or without the Adversary. We must find their every colony and every nest and destroy them. When we reach the Adversary there must not be a single agent of his behind us and we must know for certain that this war ends with him.

"This war is not about conquest, for either side. It is a war of extermination."

CHAPTER FOURTEEN

The casualties of the battle numbered a little over eight thousand. In the aftermath, the survivors marched several miles east to make camp away from the killing field. The mood of the army was strange, oscillating between sombre and celebratory.

Once the camp was set, Nuadhu had teams sent out to forage for food and water, a perimeter set up with ditches dug. Then scouts were chosen whose job it would be to ride out to the north and south and plot where the Sons of Cain had made settlements or fortifications. Only once they reported back would the rest of the forces act.

While they waited to find out where they would head next, the army spent its days drilling and practising. Nuadhu and his commanders were often among them, but they would also spend a considerable amount of time closed off in a large tent for war councils.

They still had two prisoners who they had captured from the raiding party that had left the fort before Nuadhu had taken it. Each was kept apart from the other, and bound up with sacks covering their faces during the day. At night they were each taken to a different tent for interrogation. They were kept outside of the main camp, yet once the questioning got underway their screams would carry.

One of the two was unlikely to talk. He spent his time taunting his interrogators and trying to provoke them to kill him. He would shake and thrash and cry out when being cut or hit, but never came close to offering up anything but promises to kill and rape if he ever got free. Even his name was unknown, and he was referred to as biter.

The other showed more promise. He had identified himself as Slavoj almost immediately; tall, barrel chested, with thick bristly hair and a beard which reached to his chest. He too tried to taunt his captors, but he did so with less conviction and seemed more likely to break.

Anael had never had a taste for torture, even of creatures like the Sons of Cain which had no capacity for remorse or mercy. So she would always stay away from the interrogations. However, after a week or so in the new camp Nuadhu asked her to attend.

"Why?" She asked him.

"Because he mentioned you." Nuadhu said. "By name."

When they arrived, Slavoj was strung up in the centre of the tent so that his arms and legs were splayed out in an 'X' shape. He had been stripped naked and his body was criss-crossed with welts and slashes, while his head hung forward, limp.

The other man in the tent was the interrogator, a short and skinny man currently examining different tools placed on a table next to the bound enemy. Nuadhu dismissed him, sending him scurrying outside, before picking up a blunt stick and smacking it against Slavoj's chest. His head jerked backwards and he cried out.

"Tell her."

He blinked several times, groggy. "Wha-what?"

"Tell her what you told me."

Slavoj turned and looked at her. His gaze slid over her,

and her skin crawled where his eyes went. "You're Anael?" He asked.

"Why?" She shot back at him.

He smiled, the movement of his lips squeezing blood from his facial wounds to pool inside his mouth.

"How do you know my name?" She demanded.

"How could I not?" He answered. "You are the harlot behind every Champion of Man. Every doomsday averted comes back to you, as does the death of my sire."

"A lot of your kind's sires have died at my hands. So?"

"So, Cain wasn't just my sire, he was the father of us all."

She looked at Nuadhu. "He has nothing of value to say. I'm done here."

Nuadhu hit Slavoj again. "I said tell her what you told me."

"I am." He insisted. "Who she is and what she's done is the reason that she's so important."

"Important to what?" She said.

"To His plan. The one you call the Adversary, our lord and god, has a far greater design and this campaign of yours marks only the beginning. There are seven seals which must be broken, and you are the key to all of them."

Anael's stomach tightened and her shoulders tensed. She thought that she knew what he was talking about, but hoped he was wrong. A low creature like him shouldn't know of such things. She asked him "What do you mean, seals?"

"There are seven seals," he repeated, slowly as though he was talking to a child. "The seals are the barriers against the armies of Pandemonium rising up to take the Earth, but they can be broken. When they are all gone, the reign of humanity upon this earth ends."

He wasn't exactly right, but he was too close to the truth for her liking. "What are these seals?"

"Well, that would spoil the game, wouldn't it?"

Gritting her teeth, she grabbed the stick from Nuadhu

and hit Slavoj across the head with it. "What are they?" Her voice rose to a yell, and suddenly Nuadhu's hands were on her shoulders, restraining her.

Slavoj laughed and spat. "Cain was the greatest of us all. No other can ever match his power, his ... beauty. That your Champion killed him is the worst of all injustices."

The Champion who had killed Cain was called Krésnik, and he had done so a millennium and a half ago. Yet Anael could remember the fight that had taken place in a dark cave in Cimmeria as though it were only days ago. She brought up the image in her mind, or Krésnik's hands upon Cain's head and the black flames consuming him as the Champion's magic banished him from this realm to Pandemonium.

She saw Slavoj now, in her memory. He was slimmer then, with shorter hair and no beard, but still unmistakeably the same person. She followed him in her recollection of the past, and laughed.

"His death was an injustice?" She asked. "And how did you respond to that injustice except to flee for your life? You abandoned his beauty awfully quick to save your own skin."

Slavoj roared and thrashed, tears streaming from his eyes. She hit him right between them.

"Tell me what the seals are?"

"The first was conquest. The forging of this empire in the heart of man's world. The second was war. An army of nations standing together against the forces of the Adversary. The rest of them will come in time." He smiled again and tensed.

Too late, she noticed that he was pulling his weight to the right. The bind on his left arm snapped, and he reached across to the right. He pulled his left leg free at the same time as he ripped off the bind from his right arm. But then he fell as the slack went from the bind on his right leg. In that moment Nuadhu stepped in, grabbed

Slavoj's head in both hands, and pulled.

"He wasn't going to tell us anything else." He said, dropping the severed head to the ground.

"Maybe not. But what he was saying about the seals…"

"He was telling the truth then?"

"Yes. He wasn't quite accurate; the seals bind an armistice between my realm and the Adversary's. What he spoke of, conquest and war, weren't the seals themselves but the acts that broke them. We need to find out what breaks the remainder so that we can stop it from happening."

"How do we do that?"

She shook her head. "I don't know, but…"

He put his hand on her upper arm and squeezed. "Don't worry. He was trying to unsettle us, that's all. The way that we make sure these seals are never broken is to kill the Adversary."

"I guess so." She told him. But she couldn't stop the thought of the seals playing on her mind.

After Slavoj's death, they gave the other prisoner his wish and took his head. For almost everybody else that was the end of the matter and all they had to do was wait for the word that they were moving on so that the campaign could continue. Anael, however, found it difficult to sleep and would spend her nights walking around the perimeter of the camp lost in her own thoughts.

That was where Caoimhé found her, stepping out in front of her and making her call out.

"Sorry." She said. "I didn't mean to startle you."

Anael smiled. "It's okay. It's my fault, because I was in my own world."

"Are you okay?"

"Yes, I…" She hesitated. "No. Not really." She told Caoimhé what Slavoj had said before he had died. "Nuadhu doesn't think much of it. He's still convinced that once he has defeated the adversary everything will be okay. But if his plan truly is focused on breaking the seals rather than just this war, then it might not be enough."

"I'm with you; the idea of the seals does sound like something we have to worry about. But Nuadhu has a mission to see through and he must be single minded about that. We're in enemy territory and under his leadership, so if he falters we will all feel the consequences."

She sighed. "I know. But this only makes things more complicated."

"I can help you find out whatever there is to find out about these seals, whilst we still press on with the campaign. You don't need to take the burden on all by yourself."

"Thank you. That means a lot."

"It's what I'm here for. It's difficult to make sense of, but ever since we entered the Adversary's territory, I've been getting certain...sensations. There's nothing concrete, like when I touch the hilt of a sword and can know in an instant who forged it, who wielded it, who it has killed. It's a lot vaguer than that. But they worry me, fill me with a dread I've never felt before."

"Have you told anybody about this?"

"Only Pwyll. He understands what I mean, having his own powers. But we both thought it was to be expected given what we're doing. But now that you have mentioned these seven seals, I think it might be more important than that."

"I think so too. But we can figure it out together."

"Good. I think Pwyll will be able to help us as well."

"I think it's good how close you two have become."

Caoimhé didn't just smile, she beamed. There was almost a glow to her as she said, "We are in love. When this war is over, we intend to marry. It is a shame that you and Nuadhu cannot be more honest about your feelings for each other."

Anael blushed. "I don't know what you mean."

Caoimhé gave her a quizzical look.

Anael's blush deepened. "I have been Nuadhu's mentor and trainer since he was a child and his protector since his birth."

"But you love him, don't you?"

"I..." She looked around, suddenly conscious of whether anybody else was watching.

"He feels the same way about you. It's obvious from the way he looks at you."

"Well," she cleared her throat. "Anyway, I really should try and get some sleep."

She offered an apologetic smile and hurried back to her tent, aiming to try and get some sleep. If Caoimhé was willing to help her find out more about what the seven seals where and how they could prevent them from being broken, then she suspected that sleep might be possible. The worry would still be there, but the weight wouldn't be entirely on her shoulders.

That wasn't the main thing on her mind, however, and soon after drifting off she found herself alone in an open field with Nuadhu. She kissed him in much the same sudden way as she had after the battle, and then told him that she loved him.

He pushed her away. He didn't say anything, but his face was stern and it made her heart stop in her chest. Then his face contorted and the frown became a laugh. That laughter was echoed all around and she realised that they were still on the battlefield, the dead and the survivors alike all staring at her and laughing at her foolishness.

It was still dark when her eyes shot open, her heart hammering. She turned over, tense and anxious and willing the feelings away. She didn't feel tired and thought she would never get back to sleep. But nonetheless soon she was on the battlefield kissing Nuadhu and telling him she loved him again.

This time, he said it back. Then he embraced her and kissed her, pushing her gently to the ground. She felt a stirring in the pit of her stomach and a heat between her legs as his bare chest loomed above her and his hands parted her clothes from her skin.

He stripped her naked and she tore his trousers off. They both lay on the floor, him on top of her...and a pile of bodies below them. As soon as she realised where they were, she tried to fight Nuadhu off, but by then it was too late. His grip on her shoulders was too strong. His skin was grey, his eyes red and his teeth like daggers closing in on her neck.

This time when she woke up there was light and noise outside. An awful lot of noise, like people rushing about and shouting. She picked up her sword before she went outside, but there appeared to be no attack, making the commotion even harder to understand.

"What's going on?" She asked a Roman rushing past.

"The scouts have returned." He told her. "The king has ordered that the camp be struck and we assemble ready to move on."

With that, the dreams she had just woken from were forgotten. They were still at war, after all, and had more pressing matters to attend to.

CHAPTER FIFTEEN

The village sat thirty miles to the north of the mountain that the fort had occupied, no more than ten homes in a clearing next to a small farm. Now, the farm was dead and the few animals there were gone. The surviving humans were kept in a wooden barn, shackled and used for food. The Sons of Cain occupied the houses.

The sky was just beginning to darken when the raiders came. The thunder of their horses' hooves reached the village before they came into sight, their skin dyed blue with woad and their hair pulled up in white spikes. When the occupiers came out to confront them, they howled and raised their weapons.

The battle wasn't a long one. As the horses stormed into the village, brands touched to the thatch of the rooftops. The fire spread quickly. Between the flames and the horses, the Sons of Cain found themselves corralled.

The range was far too close for foot soldiers to fight cavalry, even when those foot soldiers could leap great heights. Within a few minutes, and a few heavy sword strokes, they all lay dead and the village was one great bonfire. The human livestock were freed of their chains and led back to the camp.

There were now two separate camps under different commands. They were both moving east, but one was travelling through the north of Germania and the other through the south. Each one would send scouts to locate the innumerable villages that harboured Sons of Cain, and then would send a raiding party to take it out. The raids themselves rarely encountered any major obstacles, but the sheer number of them made progress slow.

The human prisoners they freed also slowed things down. They were kept healthy enough, unlike the wretched things that had languished in the dungeon of the fort. But they weren't strong either, having been deprived just enough so that they couldn't flee or fight back. Most were willing to join the army and march against the Sons of Cain, but they needed time to regain their strength before they could move on.

"Why are there so many of them?" Anael asked Nuadhu after several months of raiding when it became clear just how many villages they would have to deal with travelling east. "I would have thought it would make more sense for them to group together in one massive force."

"Their aim is to replace man as the rulers of this world, to colonise it." Nuadhu said. "They need settlements and a food source. Plus, the Adversary will have expected us to march straight to him, leaving them as a reserve should he have needed them."

"At least we know that there won't be anyone sneaking up from behind us then."

"Unless there are more of them hidden in mountains."

The army advanced slowly, but they advanced. Within a year and a half, they were three quarters of the way through Germania. They estimated that they had killed more than ten thousand Sons of Cain since the battle at the fort. Around three quarters of that number of men had joined their forces along the way.

The last occupied village that they raided was one of the smallest that they had yet been to, with just four huts in a circle. There were four Sons of Cain there and no human prisoners, while the huts didn't look like they had been there a long time. Sitting in the middle of them was a stone, marked with unusual symbols. Once the enemy had been killed, Nuadhu brought Anael in to look at it.

"We wouldn't have noticed it, except that the enemy closed ranks around it," the captain of the raiding party told them. "It was as though they were more determined to protect it than themselves."

Sure enough, the stone was stained with blood, suggesting that the four Sons of Cain had died upon it. What was unusual was that whilst the blood across the stone had been splashed haphazardly, consistent with wounds drawn by swords, the lines of the symbols carved into the stone were entirely filled with blood as though it had been deliberately poured.

"Do you recognise the symbols, Anael?" Caoimhé asked.

Anael nodded. "They're an early, runic form of Enochian – the language of my kind. Our tongue has evolved from this, but the Adversary and his creations still use this early, guttural form."

"What does it say?"

"It must be an incantation. 'The blood of the bloodthirsty, spilled, gives the gift of hunger.'"

"That doesn't sound good. Hunger to whom?"

"I don't know. Can you discern something, learn its history by touching it?"

Caoimhé looked wary now. "I don't know. Perhaps. But I've never touched anything imbued with magic before, so I don't know what the effect will be."

"You shouldn't do it alone then." An idea struck Anael then. "Perhaps Pwyll's abilities will allow him to act as an anchor to prevent you from being drawn into whatever magic the stone holds, if it is a threat?"

Caoimhé agreed, and so they called for him to join them. But when he came he had a different idea. "I can anchor Caoimhé so that no harm comes to her, but I can also link your mind to hers so that you see what she does. This might help you to interpret what she sees more accurately."

Pwyll placed his hands on each of their foreheads, and they also took each other's hands, before Caoimhé put her free hand to the rock.

When her hand touched the stone, Anael felt its coolness and how sticky the blood was still underneath her palm. Then there was nothing. Several seconds passed, with both women believing that it hadn't worked and able to hear each other's thoughts agreeing on that point. Then there was a jolt, as if the whole world had leaped forward suddenly.

Their stomachs roiled and their vision swam. Then they weren't there anymore. It was the same location, but it was nighttime many years ago before the wood had been cleared or the houses built. The vision they saw wasn't their own. The person whose memory they touched was a Son of Cain, strong, agile and bloodthirsty, yet right at that moment afraid.

It was afraid because of the creature that stood before it. Little more than a shadow in the darkness, but its shape was clear enough; a tall, broad figure, horned and winged. To its senses, the Adversary was overpowering. Nor was it merely his scent, for he made the air all around heat up and there was a thrill of electricity which made the hairs on the Sons of Cain's body stand on end.

"What are you afraid of, Dragomir?" The Adversary asked.

"Afraid?" The Son of Cain, Dragomir, said. "Majesty, I..."

"There is no need to lie. I can smell it in the air, taste it upon my tongue. The fear of a Son of Cain is so much richer a sensation than human fear, if less satisfying. You are afraid. Why?"

"I...my Creator, my lord and majesty..."

The Adversary laughed. The air heated up even more and sparks cracked all around them. "You are afraid of me, Dragomir, is that correct? Do not worry, I would expect nothing less – from my enemies and my subjects alike. Now, do you have the stone?"

Relieved to be dealing with the business that had drawn him there, Dragomir signalled and from behind him two more Sons of Cain appeared carrying the stone that now sat in the middle of the village. They placed it on the ground between Dragomir and the Adversary and then retreated. At this point it was no more than a stone. There were no markings on it to indicate it had any significance.

"This is the correct stone?"

"It was carved from the star stones of the Egge, in the precise manner you instructed, majesty."

"Excellent. I could perhaps have done this with an ordinary stone, but there is no sense in shirking the natural magics that exist in this world, is there now?"

"What...what will it do?"

The Adversary remained in shadow, yet Dragomir knew that he smiled at that question, and the Son of Cain's stomach tightened. "After the conquest and the war comes the famine. But famine occurs in cycles and is far from unknown by man, so this one must be a special one. This stone and the Champion of Man will be its cause, but it will spread across half the world without him ever knowing."

"How?"

"With the spilling of undead blood, ultimately. But the first step is your sacrifice."

Before Dragomir could react to those words, there was a red, leathery, clawed hand upon his chest and another on the stone. The Adversary was close enough to be visible now, but Dragomir had no time to look as fire ran through him and he screamed. He could feel it biting at his flesh and his bones, the smoke rising from his skin.

Then after what felt like an eternity it stopped and he

fell to his knees. He could feel the strength dripping out of him and knew that his end was near, even though his head remained firmly attached to his body. The last thing he saw was the stone, the runes glowing red upon it, before everything went black.

There was a pop, and with Dragomir's death in the past, Anael, Caoimhé and Pwyll were flung to the ground in the present. They cried out as they landed, then blinked as they re-familiarised themselves with their own surroundings.

Anael and Caoimhé shared a look, Anael's worry and tension written upon Caoimhé's face.

"That must be the third seal." Caoimhé said. "When the raiding party killed the Sons of Cain and their blood spilled on the stone, it activated the Adversary's spell."

"Famine. Across half the world." Anael said. She felt ill.

They went and told Nuadhu what they had learned. He too looked sick at the thought of a famine being unleashed when blood had touched the stone, but when the story was told he shook his head.

"If it is done there is nothing we can do about it." He said. "We are closing in upon the Adversary, and once he is slain he can do no more damage to our world."

Anael knew that he was right, and that there was no realistic way that they could stop a famine, even if they knew where to begin. But she still wanted to argue against him, to rail against how easily he appeared to have accepted what had happened and decided to move on.

"People are going to die." She said. "I just wish we could do something about it."

He closed his eyes and sighed. "I know, Anael. Those who die in this famine will only be the latest of far too many casualties in this war. But we cannot do anything about it and we will drive ourselves mad trying to make it otherwise."

There was a sadness in his eyes as he said it, and in that

moment all Anael wanted was to relieve him of the weight of his duty and his destiny, if only for a moment. But of course she couldn't do that any more than she could address famine.

"Famine cannot be fought with a sword or with fists of iron. I can only save man by leading us to victory in war, so that it what I must do."

They pressed on eastward, as they had before. But the village where they had bloodied the stone was the last one where they would encounter the Sons of Cain.

The next village lay empty and burnt out. Its farming field a charred blanket across the earth, its houses ashen husks, its animals slaughtered and their entrails scattered. Worst of all, the humans that had been kept for feeding on had been tied to stakes and had their hearts torn from their chests before their carcasses were left for the flames.

Each village after that was the same, the pattern very quickly becoming clear. There would be no more men for their army, no more crop or livestock for food, and no more small groups of Sons of Cain to kill.

"Now we have them on the run." Nuadhu declared. "They are retreating to join up with their larger force to make a last stand. Then we will wipe them out and the final victory will be ours!"

The army cheered when he said this, raising their swords in the air as he did. Anael made the same motion, but couldn't help feeling that everything being that easy was an unrealistic hope.

CHAPTER SIXTEEN

It was a month after the first empty, burnt out village when Anael was awoken in the middle of the night by screaming. It wasn't one person but many, maybe hundreds, from across the camp. A minute after she stepped outside with her weapon in hand to investigate, the flames roared up.

The screams had now been overtaken by the clash of iron and the shouts of battle. Like the flames, the sounds rose up in all quarters of the camp. There were armed men running in all directions, so with no other inkling of what to do Anael simply picked one and went with those heading the same way.

Fire was the only illumination in the night, the moon and stars being hidden behind thick clouds. The shadows moving around her were over long, shifting, deceptive. The roar and din nearly equalled the sounds of battle, making it hard to pick out individual sounds which might help her determine if a foe was near. The atmosphere was thick with fear, confusion and panic.

Something flashed to her right. She turned in time to parry a sword thrust. The enemy was an ally who had been startled. He shouted an apology before turning away.

Anael pushed on. She had no idea where she was going.

Another movement. This time to her left, too high to be a man. She raised her sword. It caught the Son of Cain's shoulder in mid-air. The enemy landed awkwardly. It barely dodged her downward swing after hitting the floor. But it was unarmed and not fast. She sliced open its cheek. Stabbed it in the gut. Took its head when it doubled over.

The running and shouting continued. Somebody was moving to douse the flames around the camp, and when some went out and the world became that little bit darker it paradoxically became slightly easier to see. The shadows became friendlier and less deceptive.

Another Son of Cain leapt at her, this one lower so that it would have tackled her in the gut. She sidestepped. It recovered quickly, hitting the ground at a roll and then leaping to its feet. She raised her sword and swung.

She stopped in mid swing as a dagger caught the creature in its temple and it howled. Avitus, one of Bricius's Sentinels, winked at her before twisting the blade and tearing out a chunk of the Son of Cain's forehead. As it staggered back he took the dagger to the creature's throat and started hacking.

For the next two hours, she kept moving and fighting. There weren't that many of them, but they moved quickly and silently, only revealing themselves when they had a clear line of attack. By the time the fires were out and the army had regrouped to drive the attackers out, there were more than a few casualties and Anael was aching and slick with sweat.

With the raid over, the next task was to gather up the bodies and account for the dead. By the time that was done, the sky was beginning to lighten and they knew that they had lost seven thousand people in the night.

"How did they manage to come upon us without anybody noticing?" Nuadhu demanded of his commanders when a war council was assembled.

"Our best theory is that the Sons of Cain joined our

ranks before the camp was set, in human form." Said Balbus, another of the Sentinels. "If that's the case, then there is nothing that we could have done. The Sentinels can sense Sons of Cain in human form, just as you can, Champion. But with our numbers split between the northern and southern forces, here we are but four among twenty thousand."

"Well, from now on I shall join you and your fellow Sentinels shall inspect the forces before camp is set and at least one of us shall be on each watch through the night. This cannot happen again."

"This will stop them from sneaking into the camp again," Avitus agreed, "but they must know that we will prepare for that. Any further raids will be more open, and in larger numbers."

"Yes they will be. So we will double the size of our watch and double our pace eastward. Scouts will be able to mark the abandoned villages and we will only have to detour if any more are found occupied."

The next raid came six days later shortly after dawn. This time, several hundred Sons of Cain on horseback as camp was being struck. They used slingshots to hurl flaming pitch, then harried the outskirts of the camp before fleeing.

In that attack, the casualties barely reached double figures. So in the next raid, the Sons of Cain appeared as the camp was setting up, using long spears and accompanied by their horned black dogs. This time, they were able to repel the attackers and kill two thirds of them, but only at the expense of several hundred more lives.

Progress through Germania quickened considerably, and within a couple of months they were into Sarmatia. Without the need to wait while villages were scouted or raided, the only brake on their progress was the raids, harrying them at different times of the day and night as they marched or camped. Only as their successful kills lessened and their losses increased did they finally tail off.

Not long after that, outriders reported back that there was a fort several miles ahead. Fortunately, this one must have been built by the Sarmatians before the Sons of Cain came, consisting of a wooden keep, wooden ramparts and a deep artificial moat.

Nuadhu ordered a bridge constructed which was wide enough to support a covered battering ram. While this was being laid across the moat against the gate, large catapults hurled rocks and burning pitch at the battlements to keep the archers preoccupied. They retaliated with flaming arrows.

The gate of the fort first cracked, and then collapsed entirely. After that, the battle was over quickly. Several thousand soldiers charged across the bridge, and in a quick but bloody skirmish put the Sons of Cain inside to the sword. When the last of their heads had rolled, nearly a hundred human prisoners were dragged out and the fort was put to the torch. They camped nearby, but once they were rested from the battle Nuadhu had the army marching again.

Two more wooden forts fell in a similar manner a little over a week later. This time, Nuadhu split his forces so that they could take both locations at the same time. Once they regrouped, they had three hundred additional bodies between them.

The freed prisoners didn't just add to the numbers of the army, however, as they reported that the army were within days of the main force of the undead.

"These creatures, your Sons of Cain, built a great stone fort once they took Sarmatian land." A woman with light brown skin and black hair told them. Nearly half of the freed prisoners were female, all of them trained warriors while the men were farmers who could hack with a sword if the occasion called for it. "It has an enormous keep, a deep moat and dark dungeons, and it was built by those they had killed, resurrected as slaves."

"We have encountered such a fort, in the west of

Germania." Nuadhu told her. "We were surprised to have not found more."

"They were forced to build them, because my people harried them endlessly from the east. Initially, we thought that they were invaders or outlaws, before we realised that they were our own people turned into something else. So we built an army. They repelled us in the first battle, and built their first fort to defend themselves. It was only half-finished when we returned, but the walls were built and the dead completed the keep whilst we camped outside and laid siege.

"Before we could breach the walls, reinforcements outflanked us from either side. The battle was bloody and our losses were high. I believe that our army has regrouped and has retreated to gain more numbers, but I cannot be sure. I was taken and have spent several turns of the moon as livestock."

"We have allies then?" Anael asked.

"Yes. My people, the Oiorpata, are fierce warriors. The people of Scythia stand with us, and they have considerable numbers. Together we will keep fighting until this foe is beaten, and the arrival of your people will only hasten that victory."

"Then we must re-join with the southern forces."

"Not yet." Nuadhu said. "We will send word to them, and coordinate our movements more closely than we have previously. But there is finally the chance that we may surprise the Adversary. We must take full advantage of that."

Following a long, if mild, summer, the transition from autumn to winter was all too fast and the army's movements slowed to a halt. Riders had been sent out to reach the Southern forces, with maps that the Oiorpata prisoners had helped them produce, but no matter how fast they rode they would not be returning whilst the blizzard which kept the camp stationary persisted.

It lasted for nearly two months, during which time

food was rationed to ensure that their supplies lasted. That wasn't a guarantee, however, and more than once fights broke out in disputes over rations and portion sizes.

Finally, the blizzard ended and it became far easier to hunt and forage. It was another week after that before the rider returned and reported that the southern forces had made similar progress to them. Musa, as commander of the southern forces, sent back the recommendation that they move on the next new moon to ensure that they set off together.

After four days of marching, outriders returned to report that they were almost upon the fort and that they had sighted the two opposing armies. Thus Nuadhu called a war council ahead of what would be the final battle.

CHAPTER SEVENTEEN

Anael was sat in the war council with Nuadhu and his commanders, but if pressed afterwards she wouldn't have been able to recall a single detail of it. The entire time her mind was elsewhere, leaping from memories to worries of the future to abstract thoughts and back again without any discernible order or pattern.

The face of the Adversary loomed large in her thoughts, last seen now twenty-one years ago on the night that Nuadhu was born. It was not her first encounter with him, but it had been the first for several thousand years and the one which stuck in her mind. His face that night had been shrouded in shadow, so that all she had been able to see was the glowing red of his eyes and the shape of the horns curving upwards out of the side of his head.

Now, as she saw that face, it wasn't approaching a doorway in Liuerpwl where Genovefa was giving birth. It loomed over an adult Nuadhu, laughing as he struck this way and that against oncoming Sons of Cain yet couldn't thin out their number. Eventually, however, they overwhelmed him. Rather than biting him or stabbing him they held him down.

That was when the Adversary stepped into full view, a

wide grin on his face and blood dripping down his chin. The next thing that she saw was the gore at Nuadhu's neck where it had formerly been connected to his shoulders.

"Anael..." He said. His lips moving even though he was clearly dead.

She blinked.

"Anael," he said again, from the seat next to her at the war council, "are you okay?"

She looked around. There was some argument still going on, nobody looking at her. She turned back to Nuadhu. "I'm fine." She lied.

But her thoughts drifted again, and the next time she drew back from images of Nuadhu's death and of the Adversary's conquest of mankind the tent was clearing out. Nuadhu was looking at her again, expectantly.

"Are you sure you're okay?" He asked.

She considered lying again, but then took a deep breath and said, "No. I'm sick with worry, Nuadhu. Now that we've reached this point all I can do is envision everything going horribly wrong."

"You don't need to worry. The strategy is sound, and we should have numbers on our side, so I'm actually quite optimistic about our chances."

She hit him in the shoulder. "That's not what I meant!"

"No. No, I know, but you don't have to worry about me."

"Don't I? Nuadhu, you must face the Adversary. Champion or not, that's more than any man should be burdened with. It's far too dangerous."

"It's my destiny. I was born to do this and I will succeed."

"But what if you don't?" She could feel tears welling in her eyes, and her anger at herself for that only made more tears come. "I don't want to lose you."

He put a hand to her cheek, tenderly, and brushed away the tears with his thumb. "You won't, I promise you."

He kissed her then, pressing lightly on her lips and then

with more force as she put her arms around him and kissed him back. Her cheeks warmed, though this time there was no embarrassment in her. She moved her hands down to his hips and pulled him closer to her.

Nuadhu broke off the kiss and pried himself away from her grasp as gently as he could. Before she could object, he took her hand and said, "Come with me."

Outside, the camp was dark and silent. Only those on watch moved and they stood in the distance, no more than silhouettes. Nuadhu led her the other way, through the tents and out into an open clearing. Above them, the moon couldn't be seen but in its absence the stars shone brightly. There was a light wind, cold when it touched her face.

In the middle of the open clearing, Nuadhu stopped and turned towards Anael. "This is better, I think." He said, before kissing her again.

Anael hesitated then, pulling back from the kiss. "Nuadhu..."

"Are you okay?"

"Yes. No. I just..."

He bit his lip and looked away. "I've presumed too much. Anael, I am sorry. I never meant to..."

She smiled then, and reached out a hand to turn his gaze back upon her. "No, you haven't. I was worried about this for a long time, conflicted even, but I think it's right. I am certain it is right."

He smiled back at her. "Then what is wrong?"

"Nothing." She shook her head, then kissed him again.

Her hands moved to the brooch on his cloak. She unclasped it and pushed it off his shoulders. A moment later her own cloak fell and she felt the heat of Nuadhu's hands upon her. They moved down, and she felt a spark rush through her skin as they ran over her breasts ever so briefly. He took hold of the tail of his tunic and had to break the kiss before pulling it up over her head.

The cold wind hit her bare skin and she shivered, her

nipples hardening as much from the temperature as from excitement. She pulled Nuadhu's tunic off him so fast that it almost ripped and then pulled him close to feel the heat of his body against hers.

When his hand slipped into her trousers and moved between her legs, she became suddenly and acutely aware of the heat and the wetness there. His fingers moved delicately, teasing her open and caressing her, and her whole body trembled with the sensation. She gripped his body tight and her nails dug into the soft flesh of his back. This drew a moan from him, but not one that told her to let go.

Anael's lower legs were trembling so intensely that she was only upright because she had Nuadhu to lean on. While his fingers worked he steadied her with his free hand and traced kisses down from her neck to her navel.

She put a hand on his forehead and pushed him back from her before he went any lower. "Not...not while I'm standing up." She said, in a breathy voice. "Let's lay down."

He nodded and drew their cloaks together so that she could lay down on her back upon them, and in the few moments that took she found that she missed his fingers. But then his tongue replaced them and she found herself breathing even heavier. Gasping. Finally crying out, not caring that her voice echoed across the night.

Nuadhu lifted his head and with his lips retraced a path up her body back to her face. As their lips met, his legs shifted hers apart and he entered her. He was so hard for a moment it hurt, before her wetness pulled him inside and she grasped his buttocks with both hands to pull him deeper in.

The rest was just sensations. Heat rising in their two bodies. The press of his hands upon her shoulders. The nip of cold wind at her toes. Him thrusting deep inside her, the pace and intensity growing. Blood running over her fingertips as she raked his back. Finally, a surge of fire that drew a scream from her lips and arched her back.

Afterwards, they both pulled their trousers back on and he pulled her close with one cloak draped over them. The night air was freezing, but with his arms wrapped around her she couldn't feel it.

"I think we may need to revise our strategy," Nuadhu said, "since I think the enemy will most likely have heard that."

Anael's cheeks flushed pink, but she laughed with him.

They lay there in silence then for the longest time, unmoving, staring up at the stars. In that time, Anael's worry about the following day was forgotten and for the first time in a long time she felt not the slightest hint of urgency about anything.

"I love you, Anael." Nuadhu said, after a length of time she couldn't discern.

"I love you too." She said.

Then silence again, bar the soft whistling of the wind.

"I was afraid." She told him, the words rising unbidden. "When I hesitated earlier, I was afraid of... I've been travelling your world for four thousand years, but in all that time I've simply done what was necessary, my duty. I've never... I love you, and for the longest time I was afraid of what that meant."

"You're not now?"

"No." She said, at that moment knowing that it was true.

Staring up at the night sky, while Nuadhu's heart beat in her ear, time seemed to stand still. Anael found herself wishing that it actually had, but knowing that it continued to march on towards the morning. Yet still, as long as they were awake and watching the stars there remained a chance that the morning might at least hold off.

A star shot across the sky, a long white tail trailing behind it. Two more followed it, then six, and finally an entire hail. They reminded Anael of the ones that had heralded Nuadhu's birth. Only as she watched they turned red, and their tails dripped down the skin of Nuadhu's back, blood running from where she had raked him while they made love.

She looked down and saw blood on her nails. Then they were claws, long and pointed with chunks of flesh hanging from them. She looked back at Nuadhu, now lying face up, and laughter bubbled from her throat. It came out as a low rumble that made the ground tremble and the air flare with sparks. The light was behind her and her shadow lay across Nuadhu; curved horns on her head, barbed tail and wings on her back.

She bent down and reached out, sinking her claws into his shoulder before lowering her mouth for the kill.

When she opened her eyes, it was still dark, but there were no longer stars above her. She felt a chill and her skin was covered in goosebumps. She looked around, and she saw a grey shape that could only be Nuadhu leaning over her, still naked. They were inside a tent.

"I didn't mean to wake you." He whispered. "You fell asleep and the temperature dropped quite a lot so I thought we ought to move."

He lay down alongside her and she turned to kiss him. She reached down to between his legs, but found his penis soft and limp, considerably smaller than it had been when it was inside her. She let her hand drop and kissed him again, before rolling over.

She felt his arms wrap around her and the warm engulf her. Her last thought was that she was at least wide awake now and wouldn't let the moment pass, but then the sky was beginning to lighten with the onset of dawn. In a few hours, they would be in battle, to bring this war to an end one way or another.

ACT THREE:
AT THE WAR'S END

CHAPTER EIGHTEEN

This fort was larger and covered a greater area than the first one that they had encountered. It was also built on a hillside rather than out of a cliff face. The moat surrounding it was dug thirty feet deep, filled with fifteen feet of water with iron spikes sticking out. The stone ramparts rose straight up from the inner edge of the moat, with severed heads on pikes lining the battlements.

Beyond the walls, the keep was flanked by two smaller towers. As the rising sun hit the sandstone, war horns sounded. A single long, sharp note. *Haroooooooooooooooooooooooommmmm*.

The Oiorpata led the advance, an army of fifteen thousand women. They were clad in bronze scale armour covering their chests and shoulders, scale-covered leather caps on their heads and metal greaves over their trousers. The front line carried long spears with tall, rounded shields, while the rest carried double edged longswords with shorter, circular shields. All of them had foot long double-edged daggers called akinakes sheathed at their sides.

Scythian foot soldiers, clad in similar armour but more overwhelmingly male, followed the Oiorpatan vanguard.

They were flanked on one side by Scythian archers and on the other by Oiorpatan and Scythian cavalry.

Once they were formed up in front of the fort, the war horn sounded a second time.

Haroooooooooooooooooooommmmmm.

The ranks parted and siege towers and catapults were brought forward. On wooden wheels, they were rolled to the edge of the moat whilst the army kept its distance.

There appeared to be no reaction from within the walls. No archers appeared on the walls and no alarms were sounded.

Orders were given, and those operating the catapult loaded rocks covered in pitch and set them alight. The first volley crashed into the tops of the battlements, sending stone and flame raining down on both sides of the wall. Still there was no reaction.

The catapults were moved backwards for the second volley. This one struck the walls halfway up, exploding into fireballs and leaving huge welts in the walls.

A third volley followed. A fourth. A fifth. On the sixth volley, the walls started to collapse. Still there was no response within the fort, and no sign of any enemy in the surrounding area. The volleys kept firing until a large enough section of the wall had collapsed that they could make their way inside.

A horn sounded in the distance, short and sharp. Ba-doom. Ba-doom. A chariot appeared from the direction it had come, carrying Pwyll and Caoimhé. The army's attention turned towards them, and the front line raised their spears.

However, it was obvious that they were alone and the Oiorpatan general gave the command to hold. She let the chariot pull up before the front line and Pwyll and Caoimhé dismount before she rode out to meet them, with her longsword drawn.

"Don't go into the fort." Pwyll called out.

"Identify yourselves." The general said, levelling her

sword at them.

Caoimhé raised her hands, and Pwyll followed suit. "I'm Caoimhé and this is Pwyll," she said, "We're part of an army that has marched here from the west. We have the same enemy."

The general nodded. "We do. There were reports of your movements a year or more ago, but nobody believed that you would make it this far. I am general Lysippe, and I will be more than happy to discuss our respective campaigns once we have taken this fort."

"That's why we're here."

"You think we shouldn't take the fort?"

"We took a similar fort. They tore the ground open under it once we occupied it."

Lysippe laughed. "Tore the ground open beneath it? We may be dealing with revenants here, but I have a hard time believing that."

"Then by all means send your forces in." Pwyll said.

Moments later, flaming projectiles came from within the broken walls and hit the siege towers. The fire overtook the towers quickly and brought them crashing to the ground.

"They're in there! Ready the next volley!" Lysippe shouted in response.

Pwyll and Caoimhé shared a look.

"You disagree?" Lysippe asked them, her tone scolding.

The ground shook then. As they tried to steady their footing, they saw smoke rising from within the fort and the water of the moat sizzling and steaming. A cry and clamour arose within the ranks of the army, and Lysippe turned her attention from Pwyll and Caoimhé to order a retreat. They moved back several hundred metres, whilst remaining in formation, and after the initial outcry discipline remained strong.

Then the whole fort collapsed, staggering everybody. The ground continued to shake and the ground tore open north and south of the fort to form a chasm several miles long and a mile wide, swallowing the ground where the catapults and siege towers had been. Molten lava bubbled up in the gap.

Lysippe returned to Pwyll and Caoimhé. "You were right, then. Why would they do that?"

"They have little use for fortifications," Caoimhé said, "they are here to wipe our race out, not to merely hold off our sieges to keep territory."

"So what is their next move?"

In answer to that, a war horn sounded an alarm. A moment later, from the north, a hail of arrows soared in their direction. Shields were raised but many of them were too late. Screams rose up all around them as the army turned around to face a foe attacking from the side, with the cavalry now in the vanguard and the archers at the rear.

Then the enemy archers retreated and the main attack came from the south. The first they knew about it were growls and screaming. The Sons of Cain were on foot and without armour, but this left them lighter and more agile. They sprinted at the archers and as the front runners took them down, the rest leapt high over them and into the main body of the army.

Pwyll jumped back onto the chariot and Caoimhé followed suit. She took the reins and led the horse out wide, close to the fiery chasm to gain some space. This gave them a few moments to assess the battle.

Already, Sons of Cain were everywhere. They fought in close quarters with the Oiorpatan and Scythian warriors. Swords clashed, monsters wrestled men to the ground, and fangs and claws ripped at flesh. At a glance it looked as though the Sons of Cain were mostly getting the upper hand, though Pwyll hoped he was wrong about that.

Several Sons of Cain ran out of the main battle towards the chariot. Caoimhé turned the chariot towards them and urged the horse into a sprint. One of them leapt over the horse, and Pwyll caught it with a slice to the stomach before it landed. The other jumped too late and collided with the horse. The animal faltered momentarily, but the Sons of Cain were dragged underneath it. Both enemies remained alive, wounded on the ground, as the chariot rode on.

Several Sons of Cain ran behind the chariot and leapt at the cart. Pwyll raised his sword and swiped left. The blade ran through a chest. He dragged it out and swung right. A Son of Cain shrieked as iron bit into its cheek. The third blow was clean to the neck. More kept coming, so he kept striking.

He didn't see the Son of Cain which leapt at the horse. He heard it scream as its neck was ripped open, felt it stumble and rear, and then everything twisted sideways.

Once he was flat on the ground, he took several moments to realise what had happened. He grasped around for his sword whilst crying out for Caoimhé. Amidst the other screams and cries of the battle he heard her groan somewhere close by. But before he could react a Son of Cain mounted him.

He thrashed and punched, managing to catch it in the jaw. But it didn't budge. It only pinned him down harder and leaned in towards his neck. Just before the teeth scraped his flesh something hit it in the side and it turned and snarled. The second blow knocked it off Pwyll and he scrambled away from where he had been lying.

Caoimhé was still on the ground, with one arm broken, but she had forced herself into a sitting position with a chunk of the broken chariot in her working hand to save Pwyll.

He found his sword and cut off the Son of Cain's head before it recovered. Then he grabbed Caoimhé and pulled her as far back from the fighting as he could. Another enemy came at him. He parried a sword stroke. Stabbed it in the gut. Grabbed its own sword as it dropped and used that to decapitate it. He now took both swords, ready to fend off opponents who came near Caoimhé.

"Pwyll!" She called out. "You can't hold this position!"

"I'm not leaving you!" He replied.

"Then give me a sword!" She forced herself to a standing position with a grunt, still unsteady on her feet, and with her broken arm cradled against her chest. She took a sword off him with her other hand and gasped.

"The owner of this sword has seen the Adversary. Recently."

"He's close by then?"

"He must be, he's waiting for Nuadhu to come."

"We have to warn him."

"There's no way to. We have to survive."

The enemy continued to come at them. Pwyll positioned himself in front of Caoimhé. He moved quick and deft. Swung. Thrust. Parried. Kicked and punched where there was an opening. He disarmed a Son of Cain and ended up wielding two swords again.

The numbers were too many. Caoimhé still had to use her own sword to defend herself. She struggled with her other arm a dead weight but she was capable and fast on her feet.

Pwyll overstretched trying to defend her and took a cut to his side for his effort. Caoimhé stepped away from him and shouted for him to worry about himself first. She blocked a strong downward strike and staggered. The Son of Cain put all his weight behind the sword. She shifted her weight. He stumbled. She took his head.

They found themselves back in the midst of the main battle. Around them men and Sons of Cain fought and died. Where the Sons of Cain made a kill they would often go to the ground with the victim to feed. In the thick of the battle it was impossible to watch out for foes whilst still making sure that the bodies on the ground were really dead. Those that weren't would leap up and drag a fresh victim down with them.

The sky darkened and rain began to fall. Light at first, before turning into a torrent. The ground became slick, the movement of so many feet churning the soil into mud.

More soldiers fell. The press of fighters became harder to navigate. Pwyll had to focus on enemies around him and his footing, and lost track of Caoimhé's position.

He called out her name as he continued to swing and strike. She might have heard and might have answered. He couldn't know with the wall of noise around him. Even his own voice was hard to pick out from the din.

A blade came within an inch of his face. He blocked it. A sharp kick to the groin took down the opponent. Swords from either side finished the job. He shouted for Caoimhé again. He might as well have been offering a prayer up to absent gods for all the good that it did. He cursed. Where was Nuadhu and their army?

CHAPTER NINETEEN

The fort came in sight minutes before it collapsed. Once it did, the tremors in the ground felt albeit weakly even from their position, Nuadhu ordered that the army increase their pace. It took them an hour to reach the lava-filled chasm.

On the other side, the battle was well underway and the fighting thick enough that it was difficult to discern one side from the other. However, Nuadhu's eyes were drawn to the island of smoking rubble in the middle of the lava, where the castle had been. Anael followed his gaze and saw the cave opening which led below the ground.

She put a hand on his shoulder. "Nuadhu..."

"The Adversary is down there." Nuadhu said. "I can feel it."

"If he is, then he is hiding. We can deal with him after the battle."

Nuadhu shook his head. He turned to Musa and said, "I want the chasm bridged and our forces ready to join the battle. Have the archers ready to provide cover in case there is an attack while we cross." He returned his attention to Anael. "This is something I must do alone. I am the Champion of Man, which means I must stand for man in this battle."

"Then let me come with you."

"No."

"Nuadhu..."

He kissed her, and when he pulled away she was surprised to feel tears rolling down her cheeks.

"You have taught me well," he said, "and if I am not prepared now I never will be. I will defeat the Adversary, but you must lead my army across and defeat his army."

She nodded.

"I love you."

"I love you too."

He kissed her again, and then rode away in the direction of the island.

Bridges were hastily constructed from the local forestry, wooden planks hammered together and supported by crossbeams to take the weight that would be moving over it. Shortly, they were brought forward and laid across the chasm. The rain was getting heavy by then.

Anael glanced across in the direction that Nuadhu had ridden, and saw a smaller bridge laid across to the island. She watched him dismount from his horse and cross on foot, before forcing her eyes away.

The first soldiers sent over the bridges secured them on the other side, and then the army formed up to cross. Anael led them over, still on horseback. She could hear the bridge creaking as she crossed and feel the slightest dip, but it seemed solid enough. Once she reached the other side, she spurred her horse into a charge and made for the battle.

It was a difficult situation, riding into fighting where there was no front line of enemies and the ranks of friends and foe were already so entangled. She couldn't simply ride through cutting down everything in her path so once she was into the thick of it she had to slow down. Conscious of what had happened to her last horse, she did her best not to take the animal straight over any bodies on the ground.

176

The arrival of reinforcements for man took the Sons of Cain by surprise. She moved through them with ease. Her sword cleaved left and right. Some leapt at her and she cut them down in mid-air.

As the rest of the army crossed the chasm and joined the fray the battlefield surged. It swelled like a river bursting its banks, the mud now so slick that a steady footing was all but impossible. But the tide wouldn't stop. The bridges limited how many people could cross at a time so the reinforcements kept coming in waves.

Anael didn't hear the splintering of wood or the screams. But as she turned back in the direction of the chasm whilst fighting she saw the aftermath of two of the bridges collapsing, and several hundred fighters disappearing into the lava. Those on the surviving bridges ran over faster, whilst those still on the other side hesitated. There were still two or three thousand people who hadn't made the crossing.

A Son of Cain leapt at her from the side and nearly knocked her from the saddle. As she reeled backwards she raised her sword. She jammed it in the side of the creature's head. It howled. She used her legs to heave herself back up to a sitting position. The horse kept running forward as it didn't know what else to do.

When she pulled the blade out chunks of skull and brain flew everywhere. She shoved the Son of Cain to the ground and rode on.

This time she heard the wood give. The soldiers on the bridge broke into a sprint, but only half of them made it. The rest went under with screams and shrieks. Now there were only two bridges left, but only several hundred warriors left to cross.

Anael saw Caoimhé, on her own and fending off four Sons of Cain coming at her from different angles. She was skilled with a sword and holding her own well enough, but she was in retreat and struggling because one arm was clearly broken. No matter how hard she fought and how skilled she was, she would fall eventually because the odds were against her. Anael spurred her horse forward.

More attacks came as she rode through the battle. She parried the swords easily enough. When Sons of Cain leapt she cut one down and was moving fast enough to avoid the others. Then she was behind Caoimhé's attackers.

She turned her horse and took the heads of two of them. The third caught her blade as it turned and fell hard. Caoimhé cut down the fourth amid the confusion. Then she sheathed her sword and took Anael's outstretched hand. She cried out when she bumped her arm whilst climbing, but otherwise got up okay.

"Draw. Make yourself useful." Anael said.

"Thanks." Caoimhé said. "It looks like you've arrived just at the right time."

"It's a talent. Where's Pwyll?"

"I don't know. I lost him when we got caught in the fighting."

"We'll find him."

They carried on riding. Caoimhé used her one good arm to cover their left side, giving Anael a little more leeway to scan their surroundings as they continued fighting.

Despite the influx of additional numbers, the battle didn't appear to be turning in their favour. It was impossible to guess the numbers of the enemy without a solid opposing formation and with the battlefield in chaos, yet for all those that they slew it still appeared as though everyone had a foe to face. In many cases, two or more Sons of Cain stood against singular opponents. If this wasn't the full weight of their forces, every member of their army and their species, then Anael shuddered to think how many of them there might be altogether.

The rain stopped while they were still fighting and the wind rose. The cold bit at them, sharp and cutting. Anael could feel Caoimhé shivering at her back, and she reached inside herself as though she was going to reveal her true form but in fact only drew out enough heat to warm them both up.

Within the great mass of bodies, all generating their own heat in the fury of battle, the combatants wouldn't feel the cold immediately. But the temperature was dropping rapidly, almost too rapidly to be natural, and it would affect the humans before it even touched the Sons of Cain.

"Someone is manipulating the weather." Anael told Caoimhé.

"Are you certain?"

"The temperature is dropping too fast. We need to find them."

"The army attacked us from the south, but their archers appeared from the north."

"The north it is, then."

Their breath was frosting in the air. She led the horse north, moving as quickly as she could whilst still repelling enemies. Sons of Cain continued to leap at the horse or at them atop it, and the swing of their swords was the only thing that sent the attackers crashing to the ground instead of them.

They weren't riding in a straight line and shortly came out of the throng to the east. When that happened and they were left with open space, Anael spurred the horse to a gallop and sped around the fighting towards the northern tree line.

Arrows came at them now, indicating that they were heading the right way. She moved in wide zig zags to avoid them as much as possible, though some came very close even so.

Once in the tree line, she found the archers lined up. They dropped their bows to draw daggers, but by then it was too late. She rode them down quick, then leapt off the horse to finish the job by taking their heads.

"This can't have been all of them." Caoimhé said.

"No." Anael agreed. "The rest must have joined the

battle, thinking that they only needed a few to guard here. They didn't expect anybody to come."

There was a thicket nearby which appeared to be glowing blue and green. Snow was falling from the sky, light and powdery for the moment. Anael beckoned Caoimhé to follow her and forced her way deeper into the forest.

It didn't take long for them to find it. There was an enormous pewter cauldron sitting over open flames. Around it stood three men in black cowled robes. They weren't Sons of Cain, but they were dead. They were muttering something over and over, and as they did whatever was in the cauldron continued to glow and sizzle, steam rising from it.

The dead sorcerers were surrounded by more of the dead. They looked up at Anael and Caoimhé with lifeless eyes and let out a threatening sound that was somewhere between a moan and a growl.

They charged, quick but clumsy, with arms outstretched. Anael took each of them down in quick succession before turning her attention to the sorcerers. Clearly set to a single task after being raised, they didn't even turn to defend themselves and after she took their heads she pushed the cauldron over and put out the fire. The grass sizzled as the contents of the cauldron hit it, but then the snow stopped and the temperature rose.

It was still cold, and the wind was still fast enough to howl as it ran through the trees, but now it wasn't getting colder and colder for a snowstorm or whatever else the sorcerers were trying to do.

"That's better. But it still won't win us the battle." Caoimhé noted.

"No, it won't. But it helps." Anael said. "Now, while we have some space to breathe, come."

She cut fabric from the clothes of the slain Sons of Cain and used it to first wrap Caoimhé's broken arm up tightly, then to fasten it into a sling to hold the arm in place. She then covered the sling with a second tunic and a shirt of mail taken from the dead before re-fastening Caoimhé's cloak over the top.

"It won't help if you get the arm caught or crushed, but it should prevent it from getting knocked about further in the run of the battle." Anael told her.

They re-mounted the horse and rode out from the tree line and back in the direction of the fighting. As they closed the distance they saw a shape on the horizon, a dark line coming up from the south. Soon enough that line became distinguishable as a great force of twenty thousand men. They had no banners and sounded no war horn, but they didn't need to.

"That is what will win us the battle." Anael said, pointing to where the southern forces had arrived to rejoin the main body of Nuadhu's army.

CHAPTER TWENTY

The rubble all around Nuadhu still smoked and the ground was hot beneath his feet. The rain sizzled as it hit the ground and rose up as steam. He couldn't run because the ground was too uneven and soon enough found himself climbing over hills of debris. Once he reached the mouth of the cave, he was faced with a steady rush of hot air rising to the surface.

Bracing himself against the heat, he stepped forward. Beyond the surface, the light vanished quickly. With nothing on his person to light a torch with, he moved on into the darkness with his hands out ahead of him. He stepped forward slowly and deliberately, the footing rough and uneven. Sweat beaded and ran from his forehead, his armpits and down his back. He felt uncomfortable and his head throbbed with the pain. But there was no choice but to press on.

Soon enough a red glow broke through the darkness, revealing a narrow and winding tunnel. It didn't appear natural, but it was too rounded to have been tunnelled using human tools. Something must have burrowed down here, and from the size of the hole Nuadhu didn't want to wonder what it was.

He kept following the tunnel until he was sure he was farther down in the earth than the sky reached up. He was certain by now that the red glow must have been the entrance to the underworld. Still, he carried on forward.

The ground flattened out and the walls fell away so that he found himself in a vast underground chamber. It was a mile wide and two miles long, with the red glow emanating from fires in stone lanterns all along the walls. The ceiling of the cave was lined with stalactites which glistened in the light, while the ground was smooth and flat except for in the centre.

Here, what started as a particularly large stalagmite rising from the ground grew into the shape of a creature with curved horns coming out of the side of its head and large wings on its back. Nuadhu stood watching it for a minute or so before stepping into the chamber.

"Champion." The voice echoed around the chamber.

Nuadhu glanced around, but couldn't see anybody else there. "Show yourself!" He called out.

The response was laughter which made the ground shake.

"Come on! What are you afraid of?"

"Little and less, Champion. Least of all you."

"I wouldn't be so smug, were I you! Your army will be vanquished here and your plans of conquest will die with them!"

"Will they? I wouldn't be so sure of that."

There was a flash of light in the centre of the room. Nuadhu fell back and shielded his eyes. When it was gone, it took a minute for his vision to clear. When it did, he saw that the stone image of the winged creature was gone.

"In any case, it is not the fate of our respective forces which should concern you now."

The voice no longer came from all around the room. The figure stepped up onto the now flat top of the stalagmite in the centre of the room. It was, like the stone figure that had been there before, horned and winged. Its skin was a deep, dark red and its body was tall and broad, thick with muscle. It grinned and revealed two long fangs framing a mouth full of pointed teeth.

"Adversary!" Nuadhu called out.

The Adversary sketched a bow. "How astute of you. Now, to business. You came here to kill me, yes?"

Nuadhu drew his sword.

The Adversary laughed. He raised his hands and the light in the lanterns flared up, then clapped his hands together and the flames vanished. Laughter echoed around the room.

Nuadhu moved further into the room, feeling out each step whilst listening for other sounds. Only the hammering of his heart and the rush of his breath broke the silence. He closed his eyes and tried to will himself calm. He raised his sword higher in the air, still listening.

Something struck him on the left-hand side. It winded him and doubled him over. He could feel the bruise forming even as he knelt there, coughing. More laughter rang around him.

He forced himself to his feet again and carried on moving forward. Still he could hear nothing beyond his own heartbeat and breathing. He gripped the sword with one hand and reached out with the other. He didn't know what he was feeling for or even if there was anything to feel for, but at this point it was worth trying anything.

He felt something. An ache in his skull and a tingle in the hairs on the back of his neck. But before he could make sense of it the next blow came from behind. Pain roared up his back and sent him sprawling onto his stomach, gasping for breath. When he tried to push himself up off the floor, his whole lower body trembled.

The Adversary laughed again.

"Is that all you can do?" Nuadhu bellowed into the darkness. "Are you so pathetic that you must attack me from behind in the darkness? Show yourself, Adversary!"

The flames roared into life again. Nuadhu blinked

against them, his eyes struggling to adjust. There was a shape in front of him. Hands grabbed him and lifted him off the ground. He flew halfway across the chamber, crashing into the stalagmite in the centre. Pain ripped up his back and his vision swam.

As it recovered, he looked back where he had been and saw the Adversary flap his wings to take flight. He circled the chamber, weaving through the stalactites on the ceiling, before falling into a dive.

Nuadhu barely rolled out of the way in time. Where the Adversary landed, the ground erupted and stone flew everywhere.

The Adversary turned and swiped with his claws. Nuadhu raised his sword to block. The Adversary grabbed the blade and wrenched it from his hand. He flung it away across the chamber. Then brought another fist down. Again Nuadhu rolled out of the way, but the impact hit the ground much closer to him this time.

Nuadhu tried again to get to his feet but he couldn't. Instead he tried to shuffle away on his back, while the Adversary followed him at a careless pace. He knew that he had Nuadhu right where he wanted him and had no need to panic or rush. Nuadhu knew it too.

"Can this really be it?" The Adversary asked. "An army of nations marches east, making war upon my soldiers for three years and now stands upon the verge of wiping out the Sons of Cain...and you are their Champion?" He laughed again.

Nuadhu stopped shuffling and stared up as the Adversary drew in closer. This was the first time that he had seen the enemy's face close up. Even aside from the red skin and horns it was inhuman. The brow protruded from its forehead, a knot of tight ridges that flowed up to the bald crown, whilst the cheeks and jawline were drawn in to appear skeletal.

Pushing himself up on his elbows, Nuadhu clenched his fists and tensed. He waited until the Adversary stood directly over him. Then he forced himself off the ground, crying out at the pain, and threw a fist at his stomach.

The Adversary staggered backwards. Nuadhu followed him and threw a punch at his head. This one caught his jaw. The sound echoed across the chamber. The Adversary spun as he fell and churned up the ground around him as he landed.

Nuadhu charged at him as he raised himself up. The tackle sent them both hurtling across the chamber, with Nuadhu landing atop the Adversary. He threw punch after punch after punch. To the face and to the chest. Each impact sounded like a tremor in the ground. Then he jumped up and grabbed the Adversary by the head. He spun as fast as he could and flung with all his strength.

The Adversary stumbled forward, only to skid to a halt while still standing. He turned towards Nuadhu. Not willing to give up the advantage he had, even with his whole body afire, Nuadhu charged forward.

The next punch sent the Adversary staggering backwards. Nuadhu moved with him and threw another. Then another. Another. Another. The Adversary stumbled and retreated but kept his footing. Blow after blow left him reeling. The pain in Nuadhu's limbs faded into the background as he continued with the volley.

Blood ran from the Adversary's mouth. He snarled. Nuadhu threw another fist. The Adversary caught it in a clawed hand. A sharp backhand with his other hand made Nuadhu's vision turn green and his head spin. Then he was on the ground again.

"Your name is well deserved, Iarraindorn." The Adversary said. "But it takes more than iron to defeat me. Before we went to war, my brother and I brought this universe into being. Eons before your species were even conceived, we were the reason for the stars and the planets that orbit them. Against that, what are you going to achieve with a few punches?"

Nuadhu struggled into a sitting position. The Adversary

forced him back down with a foot on his chest, knocking the wind out of him.

"You truly thought that you could do it, didn't you? That you, a mortal whose only talents are his fists, could hope to defeat a god?"

"Does it matter?" Nuadhu said. "Either way, your army will be vanquished and your empire dismantled."

He struggled to rise again, both hands gripping the Adversary's foot. The Adversary withdrew it, kicked him in the ribs, and then knelt on his sternum so that he struggled to breathe under the weight.

"You sound so sure of that fact, still." The Adversary leaned in closed. "But even if the army is vanquished and the empire is over, do you really think that is the end of it?"

He picked Nuadhu up bodily and ran him into the wall. He struck the stone between two lanterns at high speed, the shock of pain ripping a cry from him. Rather than drop he hung there, his shoulders held in place by the Adversary's hands and his feet high off the floor.

"I am kept from subjugating your pathetic world only by an armistice that was imposed upon me. To end it I need to break seven seals. The first of them broke when the Children of Cain built a kingdom for me in the realm of men. The second, you broke when you led the nations of man in a war against me. The famine which even now consumes parts of the Roman Empire, which you so helpfully brought about for me, was the third seal."

Nuadhu struggled, but he couldn't move his arms. He leaned forward. "Still four more to go."

"Yes. But –"

Nuadhu head butted the Adversary. The grip on his shoulders went away and he dropped to the ground. He hit the Adversary in the jaw. Then the side of the head. The stomach. The Adversary doubled over. Nuadhu punched him with every bit of his weight behind it. The blow sent him sprawling across the ground.

Nuadhu moved forward, only for his stomach to roil and a whooping cough to bring him to his knees. He spat up blood, his whole body trembling.

Then the Adversary was on his feet again. He grabbed Nuadhu by the throat and threw him against the wall. After a succession of sharp blows to the chest and stomach he picked him up and raised him over his head. The impact when he was flung to the ground made Nuadhu cry out and vomit blood again. Within a moment, the Adversary was on top of him again.

"There may be four seals still to break, Champion. But the next one breaks with your death."

Then the Adversary sunk his fangs into Nuadhu's neck. He cried out and thrashed, but he was pinned down. No matter what he did the Adversary's weight simply wouldn't shift. The sensation at his neck was sharp and hot. He could feel himself getting weaker as he continued to struggle, his head swimming and his heart hammering as his blood leaked out of his body and into the Adversary.

Images came into his mind. Memories from his life, frozen as singular moments, starting with ones that he previously had no recollection of. Staring up at his parents as an infant. Being presented with his new-born younger brother when he was three. Chasing Pwyll through Liuerpwl and the two of them fighting with tree branches. The faces of other children, of friends and their families, who had died with his town at Judoc's hands.

After this he saw his and Pwyll's trek to Wrikon with Anael. His and Anael's first duel with swords. Pwyll's enchantment at meeting Caoimhé for the first time. The journey into Germania with Anael. His victory over Judoc. The march eastward. His mind dwelt longer on the night before with Anael; first making love under the stars and then holding her close and feeling the heat of her body next to his as they slept together. He smiled.

His strength was almost gone. He could feel his legs shaking and his vision was off colour and blurred. He clenched his fist and closed his eyes, summoning every last bit of strength that he could muster. Death was almost upon him now and the Adversary drew his head away, triumphant in his moment of victory.

Nuadhu swung.

The Adversary's expression didn't so much change as drop from his face as he realised what happened. He looked down, at the hole in his chest with Nuadhu's fist in it, then back up at Nuadhu's face. He retched up blood, and quite a lot of it went into Nuadhu's mouth before he was able to turn his head away.

He could feel the Adversary's heart under his fingers, large and hard as a stone but with a viscous surface which made it hard to grip. He squeezed it as tight as he could, making the Adversary gasp and splutter.

More blood fell on his face and into his mouth, but Nuadhu forced himself to look up so that he could meet his enemy's eyes.

"Four seals may be broken with my death," he said. "But the rest will stand, because you die right here beside me."

He squeezed, crushing the heart in his fist and feeling the blood pour out thick as the fragments crumbled in his palm. The Adversary heaved up blood once more before rolling off him to the ground, lifeless.

Then it was all Nuadhu could do to lay back his head, close his eyes, and let the last breath of life leave him.

CHAPTER TWENTY-ONE

At the end, several Sons of Cain tried to break ranks and flee. Cheers rang out from the human side. But Anael wasn't content for that to be the end of it, and ordered them chased and cut down. The rain had just started again, light this time, and under the drizzle every one of the enemy lay dead on the ground.

Anael allowed herself to join in with the cheering then, as it was finally over. A force of men built from many separate nations stood together victorious over an army of the living dead and its plans to conquer the world. She was under no illusions that once they had all returned home their separate peoples would do anything but continue with their existing rivalries, wars and ambitions of conquest. But for now they had accomplished something extraordinary.

She and Caoimhé found Pwyll, who looked a little the worse for wear but had otherwise survived, and that moment of celebration faded. She looked back at the lava-filled chasm and the island of rubble at its centre, where Nuadhu had still yet to surface and panic overtook her.

There was still one surviving bridge left, so Anael had it moved to allow passage onto the island. Pwyll and

Caoimhé went with her but she ordered everybody else to stay back, fearing what she might find there. Her heart hammered in her chest and the dreams that had haunted her the night before ran through her head as she crossed the bridge and climbed over the rubble to reach the cave mouth.

Neither Pwyll nor Caoimhé spoke as they followed the tunnel down into complete darkness. They must both have been aware of the horrible tension she was feeling, as well as their own similar feelings, and so all three of them headed down lost in their own thoughts.

Once the red glow broke through the darkness, they followed it onward into the main cavern. They took several moments to take in the size of the room, the lanterns around its walls and the stalactites hanging from the ceiling, before they realised what lay on the floor. Not quite in unison, all three of them called out in shock.

Several moments passed where all Anael could do was stare. Her hands trembled and her heart hammered. All she could see were two dark shapes lying immobile on the floor, one of them larger and dark red coloured. She knew exactly what they were, but as she stared she denied it to herself, willing herself to not be seeing what lay in front of her or for this moment to be a dream.

Eventually she could deny it no longer and she snapped from the trance. She screamed out Nuadhu's name and broke into a sprint to reach him. By the time she dropped to her knees next to him tears were streaming down her face.

"Nuadhu! Nuadhu!" His body was scarred and bloody. His chest was still and his eyes were blank. "Nuadhu, please! Come on!" She put a trembling hand to his face. "Please!"

A hand gripped her shoulder. She looked up and saw Caoimhé, also red-eyed but composed. Pwyll stood a little behind her, staring blankly at his brother's body with tears running down his face. Caoimhé shook her head. Anael looked back at Nuadhu, his face pale and lifeless. More tears fell, but she didn't want to admit it.

"Nuadhu. Please..." She whispered.

"Anael." Caoimhé said gently, crouching at her side. "Come on..."

"No. No I won't. Nuadhu isn't... he can't be... he..." She broke down and fell on top of Nuadhu's chest, sobbing.

There was whispering behind her. Several moments later, Pwyll moved around and knelt in front of her. He looked pale and distant. "Anael, we need to do something with the Adversary's body." He said.

Anael looked up at him, then over at the unmoving red hulk that was the Adversary. "Yes." She said. "But Nuadhu..."

"Nuadhu is..." He swallowed back the lump in his throat, more tears running down his cheeks. "Nuadhu's de– he's d–" He couldn't get the words out. "We can take him out of here once we've dealt with the Adversary."

Anael nodded and jumped to her feet. She looked down at Nuadhu again, but then nodded, seizing the chance at a distraction. "Yes. Yes, we need to burn the Adversary's body."

They took the Adversary's body and moved it into the centre of the chamber. They broke a lantern from the wall, spilling the oil within across the corpse and using the flame to set it alight. While they were at the task, Anael found it easy to not think and to forget her grief, but as soon as there was nothing left to do but stare at the flame, tears caught her again.

She embraced Pwyll and Caoimhé and the three of them stood there in that empty cave for the longest time, cocooned in their own grief. Finally, they heard footsteps and turned to see more people entering the cave.

The first two people inside were the Sentinels Musa and Arvina. When she saw the scene inside the chamber, Musa called back a command to the other soldiers to wait.

Then she and Arvina headed over to them in the middle of the chamber. The fire covering the Adversary still burned as strong as ever, but the body within was charred bone by now.

"My condolences." Musa said. "This is a sad loss for all of us."

Anael bowed her head. "Thank you." She did her best to hold back the tears. "We will need his...him taking out of this place. What news from above?"

"The survivors have regrouped and the dead are being gathered from the killing fields for burial. The Oiorpatan general has invited us to join them in feast and celebration before we begin the march home."

"It is customary for such celebrations to go on for several days." Arvina said.

"I don't think I have the stomach for celebrations, of any length." Anael said.

"Nor I," Caoimhé agreed, "but the soldiers have marched a long way and put up with incredible hardship to win this victory. All of us have lost here, but at the very least we need to rest before heading home."

"Fine. Then we accept the invitation. In the meantime, can we get out of this awful place?"

So they carried Nuadhu's body and his sword out of the chamber and up to the surface. Once over the bridge to stable land, they found themselves facing the survivors of the human armies, formed up in ranks. There were thirty thousand in total, only a fraction of Nuadhu's army and of the Oiorpatan and Scythian army.

Anael turned to Pwyll and offered him his brother's sword. He wiped a hand across his face and swallowed back further tears before accepting the blade with a solemn nod. He took several moments to compose himself before turning to the assembled survivors and thrusting the sword in the air.

"The Great Adversary is dead!" He bellowed.

Cheers rang out, the soldiers raising up their own

swords in answer to Pwyll. There was some delay in the cheers spreading through the ranks as his words were repeated in Latin, Germanic and Scythian by other commanders. He waited for the shouting to die away before he spoke up again.

"My brother Nuadhu, son of Caiside and king of the Brigantes, gave his life to take the Adversary's. Nor was he the only one. Far too many of our brothers and sisters have lost their lives on the field of battle in these past three years. But their sacrifice was not in vain; not only is the Adversary gone and his attempt to wipe out our species thwarted, but the entire race of Sons of Cain who served as his army has been eradicated from this earth."

More shouting and cheering, again delayed as his words were translated.

"So we mourn, but we celebrate too. This is a great victory we have won today, and once we have buried our fallen comrades we will raise a horn of ale in their honour before we return to our homelands as heroes!"

As the final round of cheering rang out, he lowered the sword and closed his eyes. He blinked them away quickly but Anael saw the threat of tears in his eyes. She reached out and put a hand on his shoulder, while Caoimhé who had evidently seen the same thing took his hand in hers.

They buried Nuadhu, along with the others who fell that day, before erecting a camp where they could celebrate the victory. The revelry was beyond all expectations, particularly on the part of the Oiorpata who danced naked and took mates in the open air before sending them back to their own sections of the camp. Anael kept well apart from the celebrations, unable to focus on anything except her own grief.

In the days that passed, the lava cooled and solidified. The Oiorpata insisted that the entrance to the cave would be filled in so that nobody else could go inside. They were wary of it even with the Adversary defeated.

When Nuadhu's army were ready to march back west,

now under Pwyll's command, Anael told him that she wouldn't be coming with them.

"But where will you go?" Pwyll asked.

She shook her head. "I don't know. But I need to clear my head and think on some things, and I can't do that as part of an army."

"We'll miss you."

"I'll come back. Just not for a while."

"Take care of yourself." Caoimhé said.

"And you."

She embraced each of them in turn before mounting her horse. She had no destination, but for the moment that was for the best. With Nuadhu gone she had lost both her love and her purpose. Victory had wrought bitter rewards.

She spurred her horse into a gallop and rode away.

EPILOGUE

Two years after the final battle in the war against the Adversary and his Sons of Cain, Caoimhé gave birth to her and Pwyll's child during the winter solstice in Liuerpwl. The town had been rebuilt during Nuadhu's reign as king of the Brigantes and they had settled there once they had returned from the war.

It was well past midnight and the town was asleep, except for in the roundhouse where Caoimhé lay next to the fire giving birth attended by several other women and Pwyll. Outside, the ground was covered in a thick dusting of snow which shone under the light of the crescent moon and a starry, cloudless sky.

Caoimhé was panting heavily, between contractions. Above her, Pwyll was pacing back and forth and rubbing his hands together. Caoimhé went quiet as she stared up at him. He felt it, stopped, and looked down at her.

"Pwyll!"

"What?"

"Sit down!"

"Sorry." He lowered his head and came to sit down next to her.

"You've got nothing to worry about. You're not the

one pushing a child out of –" She bore down and gritted her teeth as she pushed, the sound she made somewhere between a grunt and a roar.

Up to that point, she had been in labour for almost ten hours with little progress, but now as one of the women examined her they noted that they could see the baby crowning. This led to much encouragement to Caoimhé to keep pushing.

Pwyll felt the urge to stand up and pace again, his nerves shredded. He settled for rubbing his hands together, but no sooner than he started did Caoimhé reach out and slap his hands even while still pushing. He put one hand on her shoulder whilst staring at the flames as she continued to push.

It was another hour before finally the baby was out. Squalling, it was swaddled and placed in its mother's arms so that she could finally see her child. It was a boy. She was exhausted, a smile on her face that was as much born of relief as of joy. Now that the child was out, Pwyll felt his own nerves wash away and the same expression cross his face. He put his arms around Caoimhé and just sat, enjoying that moment of tranquillity with his new family.

"What shall we call him?" Pwyll asked.

"We could name him after your brother." Caoimhé suggested.

A lump formed in Pwyll's throat. He shook his head. "No, I..." He didn't feel that this would be right, but he couldn't find the words to articulate why. "He should have his own name."

"Okay. How about Dáithí?"

"I like that as well. Dáithí it is."

Around half an hour passed before they heard the loud flap of wings and a shadow appeared in the doorway. The attending women were standing now, and the one of them closest to the doorway screamed.

Pwyll jumped up, looking for his weapons, while Caoimhé clutched the new child close. The women all retreated from the doorway. Pwyll had found his sheaths and drawn his two swords when the shadow stepped forward into the room.

It was Nuadhu. He looked almost the same as he had on the day he had died, except that his hair was longer and its natural brown instead of a lime-bleached white.

"Hello little brother." He said.

Pwyll dropped his blades, his mouth open as he stared stupidly, not believing his eyes.

"Nuadhu..." He said eventually. "How...?"

Nuadhu shrugged. "It appears that the Adversary's blood filling my mouth meant that rather than simply killing me, his bite resurrected me. As something else."

"He made you one of the Sons of Cain."

Nuadhu shook his head. "Oh no. The Sons of Cain are dead and gone. Any blood drinkers that rise now are my Children, as in me the Adversary has begun a new dynasty."

He grinned then and unfastened his cloak so that it fell to the floor. His face changed, revealing red eyes, sunken cheeks and needle teeth. But instead of turning to yellow grey as it had with the Sons of Cain, his skin became a leathery, ruddy brown. The skin on his back cracked and cartilage sprouted from it to form frames which, when his skin grew and stretched across them, became a large pair of wings like those of the Adversary.

Caoimhé forced herself to her feet and moved away to the mud wall with Dáithí in her arms. Pwyll reached down to take up his swords again.

Unconcerned by this, Nuadhu swept forward and with ease snapped the neck of each of the attending women in turn before they could flee. He then snatched his brother's swords from his hands by the blade and tossed them aside. He floored Pwyll with a fist to the stomach.

Caoimhé moved around the fire with the baby, meaning to flee. Nuadhu caught up to her and gripped her by the throat. In her arms, Dáithí started squalling.

Nuadhu snatched the child from her and she cried out, but he only placed the baby still in his swaddling on the soft ground. Then he dragged her over to Pwyll and threw her against the wall.

"Caoimhé." He said. "I should offer you my congratulations and my blessing on your marriage to my brother."

She tried to rise and with a punch to the jaw he knocked her out cold. He then turned his attention to Pwyll.

"I am disappointed however, brother, that you surrendered power when you came home. After my efforts to win the kingship of Brigantia from Judoc, you have abandoned the rule of the tribe to weaklings."

Pwyll said nothing. He could only stare up at the thing that had once been his brother, revulsion, fear and anger all fighting for dominance inside of him.

"Enough talk, then. To the heart of the matter." Nuadhu ran a claw across his own wrist, drawing blood. "Drink." He forced Pwyll's mouth against the wound.

Pwyll tried to resist, but with the angle of Nuadhu's wrist and the force against the back of his head, the blood flowed into his mouth. Soon enough, he found himself drinking freely, the warm liquid thick in his throat. When Nuadhu pulled his wrist away, Pwyll's vision swam. He felt light headed and unsure if the sensation was good or bad.

As he knelt, swaying, Nuadhu moved away from him and picked up Caoimhé. She stirred momentarily but remained unconscious. He held her off the ground by one hand around her neck, provoking Pwyll to cry out.

"No! Please!" He said. "Nuadhu, there's no need for this!"

Nuadhu sunk his teeth into her neck. This woke her up and she gasped, struggling momentarily before the loss of blood overcame her and made her resistance ever weaker. All Pwyll could do was watch, too blood drunk to move.

When finally he had finished with her, Nuadhu tore

Caoimhé's throat out so that her blood sprayed across Pwyll. As it hit him, he screamed. Nuadhu laughed.

"I am sorry, Pwyll, but this was necessary." He said. "For with my blood flowing in your veins and consecrated by the blood of my kill, you are made immortal. You remain human, but you will not age and you cannot die except by my hand."

"Why?" Pwyll managed to choke out.

"Because there are some fates worse than death, brother."

"You are not my brother!"

But in an instant, Nuadhu took on human form again. "Aren't I?" He said. "You will have all of time to ponder upon that question." He turned and left the room, strolling with no sense of urgency about him.

Pwyll leapt up to pursue him, but he made it only a few steps before his legs betrayed him and he was on his knees once more. Outside, there was the sound of wings flapping as Nuadhu evidently transformed again and took flight. Inside, close to the fire, Dáithí started to cry.

Pwyll crawled over to his son and picked him up in his arms. The child fell silent and gurgled, a happy expression on his face. This sent tears rolling down Pwyll's cheeks. His son was alive and for that he was immensely grateful. But if Nuadhu was telling the truth, not only was his wife dead but he was cursed to never age and to outlive his child.

Nuadhu's words rang in his head again. 'There are some fates worse than death.'

ACKNOWLEDGMENTS

I'm grateful, as ever, to those who read the first versions of the book you hold in your hands and helped me to refine it: Kayleigh Spiers and Fiona Fairless. You can thank them for any improvements they helped me to incorporate into the book, whilst any remaining blemishes are of course mine.

My wife Dee Dickens has my eternal gratitude not only for being willing to put up with me for the rest of her life, but in relation to this book for her incredible efforts as a reader and an editor. She is everything an editor should be: constructive, but utterly ruthless when it comes to what needs to be cut or changed, and I am wholeheartedly grateful for her help.

The incredible artwork fronting this book is the work of Keira James. As with her work on *Sins of the Angels*, I'm in awe of what she has created and cannot thank her enough. (Except, you know, by paying her – always pay your artists, as exposure doesn't put food on the table!)